THE ARABIAN
NIGHTS

A Selection of Tales

THE CHILDREN'S PRESS
LONDON AND GLASGOW

This Impression 1976

CONTENTS

SINBAD THE SAILOR

LONG, long ago, in the reign of the Caliph Haroun al Raschid, there dwelt in the city of Bagdad a poor man named Hinbad, who gained a living by carrying goods from place to place for other people; in fact, he was a porter.

Though, as a rule, he did not grumble with his lot, there were times when he was not content. One of these times happened to be, when, tired out by the weight of his load, he had sat down to rest outside the house of a very rich man whose name was Sinbad.

As the soft strains of music from the house reached his ears, and the scent of rare perfumes fell upon his senses, he was struck by the difference between his lot and that of the man whose name was so like his own.

"Why should I be so poor, and he so rich?" said Hinbad aloud; "am I not as good a man as he?"

Sinbad, hearing the words without seeing the speaker, sent a servant to bring Hinbad before him, and the poor man, fearing he knew not what, went into the splendid hall where Sinbad was feasting with a number of his friends.

Pointing to a seat at his right hand, Sinbad gave his guest a share of the good things on the table, and the meal being at length finished, "Tell me," said he, "why you were grumbling at your lot?"

"Pardon me, my lord," replied Hinbad, "I was weary and sad at heart."

"Have no fear," said Sinbad kindly, "I do not blame you for your words; but, that you may know how hard I had to work to win the riches I now enjoy, let me tell you the story of my life."

With these words he began as follows:

When I was but a young man my father died, leaving me a very large fortune, nearly the whole of which I spent in enjoying myself. At last I began to think, unless I wished to become poor, I had better try to make some more money with the little left to me, so, having bought some goods, I set sail for the Persian Gulf, hoping to sell or exchange them at a profit.

The ship called at several small islands, where we did some good trading. One day, when the vessel could not move for want of wind to fill her sails, we saw what seemed to be a little green field peeping above the water. Thinking it very strange, a party of us rowed out to it, taking some wood for a fire, and food, so that we might hold a feast.

We had all landed, and were in the middle of our meal, when we found to our horror that we were on the back of some huge sea-monster. The creature shook its great body, and lashed its tail so angrily that as many as could jumped into the boat, others into the sea, and soon all except myself were safely aboard the ship.

A fresh breeze had begun to blow, and the sails being set at once, away went the ship, leaving me still on the monster's back. Suddenly the huge creature dived under water, and I should have gone too, but by seizing a large piece of wood I kept myself afloat.

All through that day and through the night I was tossed about by the waves, but was at last thrown on to the shore of what was really an island. After a while the sun came out, warming me, and making me feel that if I wished to gain strength I must seek some food.

Dragging myself with great pain towards the middle of the island, I had the good fortune to find a few herbs. These I ate, drinking afterwards from a spring of clear, cool water.

Wishing to see on what sort of place I had been cast, I walked on until a man met me, who, hearing my strange story, took me to a cave in which were several other men. They were the servants of the ruler of the island, and had come to this part of it in order to fetch his horses back to the palace.

It was lucky for me that I met them that day; had it not been for this I should most likely have died, as I could never have found my way to the other side of the island, where the people lived, and to which the king's servants were returning next day.

They were very kind, giving me food to eat, and taking me with them when they set out on their journey. As soon as we reached the palace they took me before the king, who also treated me with great kindness. He listened to my story, pitied my sad state, and bade me stay with him as long as I cared to do so.

Now the chief city of his kingdom, the city in which I made my home, was built on the sea-shore. Every day ships came to it from all parts of the world, and I, hoping to meet someone from my own town, spent a great deal of time watching these ships, and talking to the merchants who came and went in them.

I also grew friendly with some of the natives—Indians they were, and very wise persons; but I never forgot to pay a daily visit to the king, with whose chief men I had many pleasant talks about the way in which their country and my own were governed.

Hearing one day of the island of Cassel, and of the sounds as of drums being beaten every night on the shore, I had a great wish to visit it, which I did, seeing many large and curious fishes on my voyage.

Shortly after my return from Cassel, the very ship in which I had set out from Bussorah, and which had sailed away leaving me struggling for life in the water, came into the harbour. Among the many bundles of goods brought from this vessel to the shore I saw those which I had bought, and on which my name was clearly written. But, on telling the captain my name, and that I wished to have my goods, he looked at me in surprise.

"How can you be Sinbad?" he asked, "when I myself saw him drowned. I fear you are not an honest man, though you look like one. I believe you are telling a lie in order to get these goods which do not belong to you."

I was at some pains to make him believe I spoke the truth, and, at last, on several of the sailors saying they were sure I was Sinbad, he let me have the goods.

Having looked through my bundle, I carried the very best of the goods to the kindly king, and asked him to take them as a gift. He seemed pleased with the gift, but not quite sure how I, a poor man cast up by the sea, had been able to get them.

I then told him of the coming of the ship, and the finding of my own bales of goods, on which he took my costly present with great pleasure, and gave me one worth far more in return. I next sold or exchanged the rest of my goods, and, having bidden his majesty good-bye, set sail for Bussorah, taking with me many articles made only on the island. These I sold for a large sum of money, for so much, indeed, that I had no further need to work.

When Sinbad had finished the story of his first voyage, he ordered the band to play again, and spent the rest of the day with his guests. The poor porter, who never in all his life had been so well treated before, enjoyed himself greatly, and, when the rich man, on bidding him good night, bade him come again the next day to hear more of his story, giving him at the same time a purse full of money, Hinbad was delighted at his good fortune.

THE SECOND VOYAGE

ALTHOUGH I had made up my mind to live quietly at home on the money gained by my first voyage, said Sinbad, when he and his poor guest were once more seated together, I soon tired of doing nothing, and having bought a large number of useful articles, once more set out to sell them to the people who lived on the various islands.

The ship carried us safely to several places where I sold my own goods and bought others; but one day we reached what seemed to be a desert island. No living creature was to be seen, yet there were fruit-trees and flowers, and meadows, and running streams, all of which looked so tempting, that we felt obliged to land, if only to walk a little in the pleasant-looking fields.

Having no wish to wander about with the rest, I took some food and wine, found a nice, shady spot beside a stream, ate a good meal, and then fell fast asleep, wakening only when the others had returned to the vessel, and sailed away without me.

I blamed myself over and over again for my folly, but, as this was not likely to help me much, I climbed a high tree in order to get a good view of the island. Far away in the distance I saw something white, and to this I went with all speed.

It was a curious thing, very large, very smooth, and rounded like a dome. While I stood wondering what it could be, all around grew dark. It was late in the day, and the sun would set in a little while, but the sky seemed to be hidden all at once by a thick cloud.

To my surprise this was not so, but the cloud was really a huge bird, bigger than I had ever dreamed a bird could be. I thought it must be the wonderful roc of which I had heard the sailors talk, and the great white dome must be its egg.

Thinking it likely the bird was coming to sit on her egg, I crept under it, and, as soon as she was settled, tied myself firmly to one of her big, strong legs.

Thus I lay until the morning, when the bird, rising high, carried me so swiftly through the air that I became dizzy, and lost my senses. On coming to myself some time later I was lying on the ground, but still tied to the leg of the huge bird.

Not wishing to go through such a terrible journey again, I made haste to get free from the bird's leg, and it was well I did so, for almost the next moment she seized a huge serpent in her bill and flew away.

I could not tell where she had carried me. All around were mountains so high that they seemed to touch the sky, and so steep that no one could climb them. I was no better off here than on the island. Suddenly I forgot my trouble for a time, for, looking at the ground, I found it was covered with diamonds, big shining diamonds.

But, alas, there were other things besides, things that filled my heart with fear, and made me wish more than ever to find some way out of the lonely valley. These were serpents, so large that they could swallow an elephant quite easily.

As the day grew brighter, however, they hid away in their homes, for fear, I supposed, of the roc, but when the night drew near they came out again in large numbers. Feeling it would be dreadful to spend the long dark night in terror lest I should be swallowed by one of the great creatures, I looked about for some place in which it might be possible to take shelter till the day dawned.

At length I found a cave, the entrance to which was so small that I could block it with a large stone. Though now feeling safer I could by no means sleep; the hissing of the serpents outside was too fearful.

As soon as it was light I left the cave, and walked a short distance through the valley, feeling far too miserable to touch the diamonds under my feet. The food I had brought from the ship kept me from starving, but I was so weary that at last I felt obliged to lie down and sleep.

Hardly had I begun to doze, however, when I was startled by something heavy falling near me. Opening my eyes quickly I saw a large piece of raw meat lying at my feet. Another piece fell, and another, and several more, and as they fell heavily upon the diamonds, the lovely stones stuck firmly into the meat.

This made me think again of the sailors' stories, and I knew that the meat was being thrown into the valley by men on the mountains, in the hope that it would be fetched back by the eagles to feed their young ones, when the diamonds could be taken from their nests.

Now I thought I could see a way of escape by tying a piece of meat firmly to my back, and waiting till an eagle carried me up out of the dreadful valley. This I did, but not until I had first filled my bag with the precious stones.

I had not long to wait. One of a number of eagles, picking me up, bore me to his nest on the top of the mountains, where I was found by a merchant who had frightened the eagle away. At first he looked at me in surprise, and then said I had no right to steal his diamonds.

"If you will listen to me," I said gently, "you will find I am no thief, though having enough diamonds to make both myself and you rich for life. I got them from the valley, and chose the very best to be found."

The other merchants now crowded round, and all showed great surprise at my story. They wondered much at the trick I had played, but they wondered still more when I showed them the stones.

Though I begged him to take several, the merchant who had found me would take only the smallest of them, which he said was a good fortune in itself. They agreed to let me spend that night in their camp, which I did, and was then taken to the merchant's house, where I told my strange story again to his wife and children.

In the course of time I once more reached my home, and settled down to a life of ease, and made glad the hearts of my poor neighbours, by sharing my riches with them.

This being the end of Sinbad's second story, he gave Hinbad another purse of money, and asked him to return the next day.

THE THIRD VOYAGE

My THIRD voyage, said Sinbad the next day, was hardly begun when a very great storm arose, and the captain told us the ship was being driven towards an island, which was the home of numbers of little hairy savages not more than two feet high. He said they were very fierce, and we had better not make them angry.

As our vessel neared the land a swarm of them swam out, dragged it ashore, made us all get out, and then took the ship away with them to another island. As it was useless to stand and look after them, we walked on until we reached a beautiful palace, the courtyard of which we entered.

The yard led to a room where we saw a heap of men's bones, and a large number of spits, or long, steel skewers, on which joints of meat are roasted. As we stood looking at these things, a truly terrible ogre came into the room, making a loud noise.

In the very middle of his forehead was a huge eye, the only one he had; his mouth was like that of a horse, and his ears flapped down on his shoulders like an elephant's. He was as tall as a high tree, and one glance at him was enough to make us all nearly die with fright.

Having taken a good look at us, the horrid ogre picked me up by my neck, and turned me round and round, but seemed to think me too thin, for, indeed, I was little more than skin and bone. Then he seized the captain, who was the fattest of us all, stuck a spit through his body, roasted, and ate him.

After this he went to sleep, and troubled us no more till the next day, when he roasted and ate another of our crew. On the third day he ate another, and we then made up our minds to kill him and try to escape. There were ten of us left, and each one taking a spit, and making its point red hot, we stuck them all together into the one eye of our terrible enemy.

Mad with pain he tried to seize us; but we got out of the way of his fearful claw-like hands, and ran off to the shore. Here we made some rafts, but had not got afloat when two giants came in sight leading the terrible ogre who we had fondly hoped was dead.

Jumping on to the rafts we pushed off from the shore; but the giants, wading into the water as far as they dared, threw after us some huge stones which, falling upon the rafts, sank them all but the one on which I stood with two other men. Happily we got out of their reach quickly, and, after beating about on the sea for many hours, came to another island, where we found some very good fruit.

Being now tired out we lay down to sleep, but were soon awakened by a rustling sound which, to our horror, we found was made by a huge serpent. Before we could get away, the creature swallowed one of my comrades, and then went back to his den. The next night he came again, and caught the second of my comrades, as he was following me up a tree, where he had hoped to be quite safe.

In the morning, feeling very miserable, I made up my mind to drown myself, but, on reaching the shore, I saw some distance off a ship passing slowly by. Unrolling my turban I waved it aloft, shouting loudly the while, until the captain sent a boat to fetch me to the ship.

Good fortune now met me once again, for this was the very captain who had sailed away without me on my second voyage. As soon as he learned who I was, he told me how glad he was to have been able to make up for that fault, by saving me now from what might have proved a worse fate.

He had taken care of my goods left on the ship, and now returned them to me with much pleasure. On reaching port I sold them at a fair price, and again returned to Bussorah with a large sum of money.

From Bussorah I went to Bagdad and bought another fine house with splendid grounds all round it. As I had done each time before, so I did now, giving a great deal of money to poor people of the city, and settling down for some time to a quiet life. But this I found very difficult to do, and at last went to sea for the fourth time, when again many wonderful things befell me.

Hinbad went home that night with a glad heart, for he was no longer poor. In his hand he held a purse of money, and it seemed as if his rich friend meant to give him the same, every day he spent with him.

THE FOURTH VOYAGE

As soon as dinner was over, Sinbad began the story of his fourth voyage. Having set all my affairs straight, he said, I travelled through a great part of Persia, buying and selling. At last, reaching the coast, I went aboard a ship, which, after calling at several places on the mainland, stood out to sea.

But soon a great storm arose; the sails were torn in shreds, the ship was blown upon the land, and many of the passengers and sailors were drowned.

With a few of the others I clung to a plank, which was washed ashore on an island, where we found fruit and water, of which we ate and drank freely. The next morning we set out to explore the island, but before getting far were met by some black men who carried us to their homes.

They seemed very kind and gave us a tasty herb to eat.

Though feeling as hungry as my comrades, I ate none of this herb, fearing it might do me some harm. In this I was wise, for I was the only one who kept his senses. The others became dazed, and ate freely of the rice with which they were daily fed, becoming at last very fat, when the black men killed and ate them.

The horror of the whole thing, together with the very little food I ate, kept me so thin that the blacks took no notice of me, which gave me the chance of going here and there without being watched. One day, when all the people except one old man had gone out, I walked slowly till some distance away from the village, when I set off running as fast as I could, taking no heed of the old man's cries.

Resting a while now and then, I hurried on until night came. For seven days I met no one; on the eighth I had the good fortune to come upon some white men gathering pepper, which was plentiful on the island. On hearing my story they seemed very much surprised that I had got away with my life.

They treated me with much kindness and, when their work was done, took me with them to their own island, where the king gave me some new clothes, and bade his people take great care of me. I became a great favourite with everyone, and at last found a way of paying back a little of their kindness.

Seeing that all of them, even the king, rode upon the bare backs of their horses, I thought out a plan for making a saddle and bridle and stirrups. This, with the help of two workmen, I did, and gave the first set, when finished, to the king. So many costly presents were given me by those for whom I made saddles that I was soon a rich man again.

One day the king, as a token of his love, gave me a wife, thinking I should be more likely to settle down in his country, and not wish to return to my own. At first I was pleased enough to stay, but after a time I began to long for my own home in Bagdad. Therefore, keeping my eyes open, I waited for a chance to escape, which came about in a very curious manner.

My wife, who for some time had not been strong, fell sick and died, when, according to the custom of the country, I was buried with her in a deep pit on the side of a mountain near the sea.

My coffin was an open one, and when the mouth of the pit had been blocked by a huge rock, and the king with the other mourners had gone away, I rose, and by the aid of a little light that came through the corners not quite covered by the stone, looked about me.

The pit or long cave, as it really was, seemed full of dead bodies, which smelt so horribly that I was forced to hold my nose. At first I wished I had died in one of the storms at sea; then I was filled with a keen desire to live. Taking some of the bread and water placed in the coffin, I groped about to find some outlet from the cave, but failed to do so.

My food was nearly all gone, when, one day, the mouth of the cave was uncovered, and I saw another burial taking place. The dead body was that of a man, and his wife being buried with him, the usual seven small loaves and a pitcher of water had been placed in her coffin. The poor woman, however, soon died, so I took the bread and water, which lasted me for several days.

Then, one morning, hearing a strange sound, I was able to follow it, until I came upon an opening in the cave, through which I crawled, and found myself on the sea-shore. The sound I had heard proved to be the heavy breathing of some creature that had come into the cave to feed upon the dead bodies.

Feeling sure now of being able to get away from my living tomb, I went back to the cave in order to get the precious stones, and jewels, and costly stuffs buried with the dead bodies, and also to bring away my bread and water. On again reaching the shore I made several neat bundles of the goods, and then settled down to wait for the passing of some ship in the hope of being picked up.

On the third day, a vessel sailed slowly out from the harbour, and I, waving the linen of my turban, shouted loudly, which at last caused the sailors to look toward me. In a few minutes a boat was lowered and the three men rowed ashore to fetch me.

To account for being in so strange a place, I told them I had been shipwrecked, but had got safely to land with a portion of my goods. The story was really a very poor one, but they seemed not to notice it, being far too busy with their own affairs.

The ship called at several ports on the islands and the mainland, where I made another large fortune by the sale of the articles brought from the cave, and at length I reached my home in safety.

As an act of thankfulness for having come safely through my troubles, I gave large sums of money to the church, to the poor, and to my own kindred, who listened in wonder to the story of my latest adventures.

Here Sinbad wished his guests good-night, bidding them all dine with him next day, and giving Hinbad the usual purse of one hundred sequins.

THE FIFTH VOYAGE

THE pleasures of my home, said Sinbad the next evening, made me forget past dangers, so, when the longing for travel came upon me, I bought many costly articles with which to carry on my trade, and sent them to the seaport town where a vessel was being built for my use.

The ship being larger than I needed for my own goods, I agreed to take several other merchants with me, and we set out in great hope of doing good business at the ports where we meant to call.

But, alas! coming one day to a desert island,

where we found a young roc just ready to break from its shell, the merchants roasted and ate it, and thus brought about the deaths of everyone except myself.

Just as my comrades had finished their meal, for I would by no means join in it, we saw the parent birds coming. The captain, fearing the anger of the great creatures, who looked like two large clouds floating in the sky, hurried us aboard and sailed away with all speed.

As soon as the old birds found what had been done, they swept down with a great noise, took up two huge stones, and flew after us. Stopping just above us they dropped the stones, one of which fell upon the ship, smashing it in pieces, and killing most of the sailors and merchants. Some, myself among them, sank into the water.

On coming to the surface I caught hold of a plank with one hand, and swam with the other, changing them at times, until the tide carried me to an island, the shore of which was so steep that some further toil was needed before I reached a place of safety.

In the morning, after eating of the fruits which grew in plenty, and drinking of the fresh, cool water of a brook, I wandered about, looking with pleasure at the beauty of the place.

After a time I saw a little old man making signs to me to carry him on my back over the brook. Having pity on his age, I did so, but, when I would have pulled him down on the other side, he twisted his legs so tightly round my neck, that I fell to the ground half choked.

Though he saw how faint I was he made no sign of getting off, but, opening his legs a little to let me breathe better, he dug his feet into my stomach to make me rise and carry him farther. Day after day, and night after night, he clung to me, until by good luck I got rid of him in the following way.

Coming to a spot where, a few days before, I had left the juice of some grapes in a calabash, I drank the juice, which in the meantime had become very good wine. This gave me fresh strength, and, instead of dragging myself wearily along, I danced and sang with right good-will.

The old man, seeing how light-hearted the wine had made me, signed to me to give him some. He took a deep drink, and soon became so merry that he loosed his hold on my shoulders, when I tossed him off, and killed him with a big stone, lest he should make me his victim once more.

Some sailors whom I met shortly afterwards, their ship having put into the island for water, said I was the first person they had ever known to escape from the old man of the sea, who for years had been a terror to those obliged to visit the island.

One of the merchants on board, taking pity on my state, gave me a large bag, and advised me to go picking coconuts with some men whom we met in a place much visited by foreign traders. I kept close to the party, as he had bidden me, until we reached the place where the coconuts grew.

The trees were so tall that I wondered how we should get the nuts, when the men, picking up some stones, threw them at the monkeys of whom there were many on the branches. These creatures, in return, pelted us with coconuts, throwing them down so quickly that we soon filled our bags.

Day after day this was done until at length we had enough to fill the ship which waited for us in the harbour. Then, bidding the friendly merchant good-bye, I went aboard, and in due time arrived in Bagdad, none the worse for my adventures. I had done well, too, with my coconuts, having changed them for pearls and spices in the places at which we had called on the voyage.

Giving Hinbad another hundred sequins, Sinbad wished him good night, and asked him to return next day to hear the story of his sixth voyage.

THE SIXTH VOYAGE

You will perhaps wonder why, after meeting with so many dangers, I should again venture forth, when I might have stayed quietly at home, said Sinbad, taking up his story where he had left off the day before. I wonder myself, now, yet at the time I was quite willing and eager to set out.

Travelling by way of Persia and the Indies, I at length took passage on a vessel bound on a long voyage. After being many days at sea the captain and pilot lost their way. They had no idea where we were, until the captain found his ship had got into a most dangerous current which, unless God took pity on us, would surely carry us to our death.

Almost mad with grief he left his place on deck, and went to see that his orders were carried out; but, as the men set about changing the sails, the ropes broke, and the vessel, now quite helpless, was carried ashore and wrecked, yet not so badly, for we were able to save our lives, our goods, and our provisions.

But even such comfort as was left us was taken away by the captain. "We may as well set about digging our graves," said he, "for no one ever escapes from this terrible place."

And, indeed, this seemed true, the shore being covered with wrecks, and goods of great value, and, worst of all for men in our position to see, the bones of those who had already died there, as we were only too likely to do.

The coast was very steep, and there seemed no way of climbing up, but under the hills, through a great cave, ran the very current that had brought us ashore. For some days we wandered about, heedless of the precious stones under our feet, thinking only of our sad fate. The most careful ate only a little of their share of food each day, so that some lived longer than others; but at last I was the only one left, and, wild with grief at my folly in leaving home, I began to dig my grave, fully believing that now at least there was no more hope.

Yet it pleased God again to spare me. As I stood, lonely and miserable, looking upon the currents that had wrought our ruin, an idea came into my head. With all speed I made a raft with the pieces of timber on the shore, loaded it with the precious stones and costly stuffs lying here and there, and stepped aboard, trusting that the stream would carry me to some place where men lived, and so give me a chance of escape. If I lost my life, I should be no worse off than in staying on the coast to die.

With two small oars I guided the raft, leaving it to be carried by the current. Several days passed, and still the raft floated on in total darkness through the long tunnel. At length my food being all eaten, I sank down in a state of drowsiness, and awoke to find myself once more in the light, and surrounded by a number of black men.

Full of joy at my good fortune I rose, and gave thanks aloud to God, who had brought me to a place of safety. One of the blacks, understanding my words, stepped forward and asked how I had reached their country. They had seen my raft floating in the river, he said, and had tied it to the bank till I should awake. After eating a little food I told them of my strange adventures, the man who had first spoken to me telling the others what I said, he being the only one who understood my speech.

They looked at me in wonder, and placing me on a horse took me straight to their king. He thought my story so strange that he had it written down in letters of gold, and put away with the important papers of the kingdom. The sight of my raft and bales of goods, which the natives had taken care to bring with them, was a still further surprise. He thought my treasures very beautiful, but most of all the emeralds, of which he himself had none.

Seeing this, I begged him to accept the whole of my goods, as a token of my thankfulness to him and his people, but this he would by no means do. He said that instead of taking my riches he meant to add to them, and meanwhile, I was placed in the care of one of his chief men, who treated me with great kindness.

Though the time passed pleasantly, I could not but long to return to my home. Going therefore to pay my daily visit to the king, I told him of my wish, and begged that he would let me return to Bagdad. He agreed at once, and, giving me many valuable gifts, asked that I would carry a message of friendship to the Caliph Haroun al Raschid, together with a costly present, and a letter written upon a skin of great value. Then, sending for the captain in whose ship I was to

sail, and the merchant who was to travel with
me, he charged them to treat me well on the
journey.

Reaching Bagdad in the course of time, I set
out to fulfil my promise to the king. His gift to
the Caliph was made up of four things—a beautiful cup cut out of a large ruby and filled with
pearls; the skin of a serpent supposed to keep
anyone who lay upon it from becoming ill; a
large quantity of wood of aloes, and of camphor;
and a beautiful slave whose clothing was rich
with jewels.

The Caliph, astonished at the richness of the
gift, could not keep from asking many questions
about the king who had given it into my care.
After telling him all he wished to know, I was
free to return home, and to settle down again,
this time, as I thought, for good.

The story being finished, Hinbad went away,
taking with him another purse of gold; but the
next day he returned to dine with Sinbad, who,
after the meal, told the story of his seventh and
last voyage in these words.

THE SEVENTH VOYAGE

I WAS one day enjoying myself with some friends,
when a slave from the palace came with a message
that I should go to the Caliph at once. His High-

A.N.   B

ness, having written a reply to the letter from the King of the Indies, wished me to carry it to him, together with a suitable present.

Now, though it would have given me great pleasure to serve my sovereign in any other way, I felt quite unable to face again the dangers of the sea, and, to let him know why, I told him of all the misery through which I had passed. In reply he said that though he felt very sorry for me, yet I must bear his letter and gift to the King of the Indies.

"You have but to sail to Serendib," said he, "and present my gifts to his Majesty: after that you are free to return to Bagdad."

Seeing that he would not change his mind, I at last agreed to go, and, after a fair and pleasant voyage, arrived at the king's court. The gift was a very costly one, and his Majesty showed great pleasure when it was handed to him.

After a short stay in the island I begged leave to depart, but the king gave his consent only after much pressing on my part. I went on board the vessel, taking with me a splendid gift, and hoping to have a speedy and pleasant voyage.

We had been at sea, however, only about three days, when the ship being seized by pirates, I was taken with several others and sold as a slave. The rich merchant, who bought me, treated me well, and, finding I was able to shoot with a bow, took me out with him to shoot elephants of which there were numbers in the forest.

Having told me to climb a tree and to wait for the animals to pass by, he gave me a supply of food, and went back to the town.

No elephants passed during the night, but in the morning I shot one out of a large herd. As soon as the others had gone, I ran quickly to my master, who, praising me highly, came back to the forest and helped to bury the huge creature. This he did in order to get the tusks, when the flesh had rotted away from them.

Every day for two whole months I shot an elephant; then one morning, as I waited in the tree for them, instead of passing by they came towards it, and looked at me steadily for a few moments. I trembled with fear, for the creatures were many in number, and seemed bent on taking my life in revenge for the death of their friends.

One great animal at last tore up the tree in which I was by the roots, lifted me from the ground where I had fallen, placed me on his back, and, closely followed by the others, carried me to a field, some distance away, which I found afterwards to be covered with the bones and teeth of dead elephants.

Having laid me on the ground they all went away, leaving me lost in wonder at their wisdom. It seemed as if they knew it was only their teeth I wanted, and they had brought me to their burying-place, so that I could get all I wished without killing any more of their number.

Here, indeed, was a great treasure, and I went

quickly to tell my master of my good fortune. As I met no elephants on the way, I felt sure they had gone farther into the forest in order to leave the road open. My master, wondering why I was so long away, had meanwhile gone to the tree and found it torn from the ground, so he was overjoyed to see me, having feared the creatures had killed me in their anger.

The next day we rode to the spot on an elephant whom we loaded with as many tusks as it could carry, and on getting back home my master said that as he had become a rich man through me, I should be a slave no longer.

"The merchants of this city," he said, "have had many slaves killed by the elephants, who are indeed very cunning animals. But it has pleased God to spare your life, and to show how every one of us may become rich without the loss of any more lives. I have no doubt that when the people of this city hear about this they will all wish to help in making you a rich man, but I would rather do this by myself. I will not only set you free, I will give you enough money to live on for the rest of your life."

Having thanked the merchant for his kindness, I said, "Sir, I have no wish to take so great a gift from you. Give me leave to return to my own country a free man, and I shall be well content."

This he was quite willing to do, saying that as soon as the wind was fair, he would send me home in one of the ships that would then come to carry away the ivory.

While waiting for the ships I made several journeys to the hill with the friendly merchant, bringing home so many tusks that the storehouses were soon full of ivory. The vessels came at last, and the merchant himself, choosing the one in which I was to sail, filled it with ivory, the half of which he said was mine. Besides this splendid present he gave me a number of things found or made only in that island, and enough food to last the whole voyage: he also paid the cost of my journey.

The voyage was a good one, yet, knowing the dangers of the ocean, and how quickly storms arise, I landed at the first port we reached on the mainland, taking with me my share of the ivory which soon sold for a great deal of money.

Having bought some rare gifts for my family, I set out for Bagdad with a party of merchants. The way was long and tiring, but reaching the city at length, I went straight to the Caliph, in order to let him know that his commands had been properly carried out.

I had been so long away that he feared some danger had befallen me, so I made bold to tell him of my adventures. The story of the elephants filled him with wonder; indeed, had he not known me to be a truthful man, he would not have believed it.

As it was he gave orders that this story, as well

as all the others I had told, should be written in letters of gold, and kept in a safe place for all time.

My family, my kindred, and all my friends welcomed my return with great joy. Since that, my last voyage, I have lived a quiet life, doing much good.

"Now, friend," he added, turning to Hinbad, "I think you will agree I have earned the riches I enjoy, and the pleasures that fill my life."

THE STORY OF ALADDIN, OR THE WONDERFUL LAMP

IN ONE of the large cities of China there once lived a tailor, whose name was Mustapha. Mustapha was very poor, and he found it hard to provide food for himself, his wife, and his only child, Aladdin.

Aladdin was a very naughty and lazy boy. He would never do what his parents wished him to do, but played in the streets from morning till night with boys who were as naughty as himself.

When Aladdin was old enough to learn a trade his father took him into his own shop and began to show him how he should use the needle. It was of no use. Aladdin had had his own way so long that now he could not settle down to work. His father tried him over and over again, and was at last so vexed at his son's idle habits that he became ill and soon died.

The poor widow thought that surely now her son would earn a little money. But no. Aladdin was as idle as ever. In despair, the good woman sold all the things that were in the shop, and with the money and a little she could earn by spinning cotton she got on fairly well.

One day when Aladdin was playing in the street

with some more boys, a stranger saw him and stopped to look at him.

This stranger was a magician, and as he looked at Aladdin he said to himself, "This is just the kind of boy I want. He is daring and bold, and will just suit me." Going up to Aladdin he drew him aside from his playmates.

"Is your father called Mustapha?" the magician asked quietly. "And is he not a tailor?"

"Yes," replied Aladdin, "but he is now dead."

Hearing this, the stranger threw his arms around the boy and kissed him, while tears seemed to flow down his cheeks.

Aladdin asked him why he wept. "Alas!" replied the stranger, "how can I help it? I am your uncle. Your father was my brother. I have tried to find him all over the world, and now I have come too late."

The stranger then asked Aladdin about his mother, and, putting some money into his hand, bade him go home and say he would call to see her next day.

Aladdin ran off with glee.

"Mother," said he, "my uncle found me in the street to-day, and he bade me tell you he is coming here to-morrow."

"Your uncle found you?" asked the good woman. "Nonsense; you have no uncle."

"At any rate, a stranger hugged and kissed me, and gave me this gold," replied Aladdin. "He surely *must* be my uncle."

Aladdin's mother did not know what to think. She had never heard of this uncle before; but, as Aladdin then went out, nothing more was said.

Next day the stranger again saw Aladdin playing in the street. "Here is some more money, boy," said he, kissing him again; "take it to your mother, and tell her to buy some things for to-night's supper. I shall call on you then."

Aladdin took the money home, and, though his mother could hardly believe her senses, she spent the money in buying good food for supper. As for Aladdin, so eager was he to see his uncle once more that he went out into the street to show him the way to the house.

The stranger came. He brought some bottles of wine and some nice fruit. When these had been set on the supper table he said to the widow, "Pray, show me the place where my poor brother used to sit."

She showed him the corner of the sofa.

At once the stranger fell down before the place and began to kiss the sofa. "My poor, poor brother," said he. "How I should like to see you! But I am too late! Too late!"

After a while the three sat down to supper and had a good meal. Then they talked, and the stranger said what joy it would give him to set Aladdin up in a shop, so that he might earn a good living by the sale of goods.

In the course of the next few days the stranger brought Aladdin some new clothes and took him into the rich parts of the city. Aladdin was proud to be seen in fine clothes, and thought his uncle a very kind man. "To-morrow," said the uncle to Aladdin, "I will show you some finer sights than these. Be ready for me early."

Morning came, and the two set out through the city gate. Their way led them past some large palaces with beautiful gardens round them, through which they walked. Each one was more handsome than the other, and Aladdin was full of joy on seeing them.

At last both were tired. "Let us sit down here," said the uncle to Aladdin. "I want to offer you some good advice, before I let you have the shop."

"How much farther are we going?" asked Aladdin. "I fear I cannot walk back unless we turn soon."

"Take courage, my dear boy," said the uncle. "I wish to show you one garden more which is better than all the others we have seen. You are rested now. Let us go on."

Soon they came to a narrow valley where all was quiet. "This is the place I wished to reach," said the uncle. "There are wonders here which you have never yet dreamt of. I am now going to strike a light, and you must gather me some dry sticks in order to make a fire."

There were plenty of sticks near at hand, and soon Aladdin had a large heap of them. The uncle then set them on fire, and, as the blaze grew, he threw perfume into it, and spoke some strange words.

Aladdin began to feel afraid, and thought of taking to his heels. Just at that moment, however, the ground beneath them shook, and there came into sight a square stone about a foot and a half across, with a brass ring fixed right in the centre for the purpose of lifting it up.

"You have seen my power," said the uncle to Aladdin. "I want you now to do something for me."

Aladdin, though he shook with fear, said he was quite ready to do all that was wanted of him.

"Then pull that stone up by the ring," said the uncle. "It will come up easily enough if you repeat the names of your father and grandfather."

Aladdin took hold of the ring, and, strange to say, was able to lift the stone without the least effort.

"The next thing to do," went on the uncle, "is to go down that well. When you come to the bottom go through the door into a large hall; then through many halls one after the other, keeping a straight course, till you come to where you will find a lamp burning in a niche of the wall. Bring the lamp to me."

As he spoke these words he put a ring on Aladdin's finger, saying, as he did so, that it would keep him from all harm.

Then Aladdin went down the well, and found all things as the uncle had said. There were the halls, and there were gardens too, with trees in them, which bore strange-looking fruit of all colours—red, white, blue, and so on. They were, in truth, precious stones of great value.

When Aladdin came to the lamp he took it down from the wall, and, having put out the flame, carried it in his bosom. He took also some fruit from the trees, and at last came to the bottom of the well.

Up the steps he went, and saw the stranger outside waiting for him. "Give me the lamp," said the uncle; "you will be able to get out more easily."

"No, no," said Aladdin. "Help me out first, and then I will give you the lamp."

Now, I must tell you that it was the lamp the stranger wanted. He was not the real uncle of Aladdin, but had taken these means of getting it, for he alone knew where it was. He had come all the way from Africa for it, and was in a sore plight when Aladdin would not give it to him.

The stranger tried all the means he could, but Aladdin had sense enough not to part with the lamp. Seeing this, the stranger added a little more perfume to the fire, which he had all the time kept up. Then he said two magic words, and lo! the stone which had covered up the well, and kept it from view, flew back to its place of its own accord. Then he made off as fast as he could to Africa.

Aladdin, of course, knew now what to do. He cried out many times that if his uncle would take away the stone the lamp should surely be his. But the stranger was now a long distance off, and all Aladdin's cries were in vain.

For two full days Aladdin lay helpless in the well, without either eating or drinking. On the third day, when he had quite given up all hopes of ever seeing daylight again, he joined his hands together, as he would have done had he been saying his prayers.

As he did so he chanced to rub the ring which the stranger had put on his finger.

The next instant a genie, tall and strong, stood before him. "What do you wish?" said the genie. "I am ready to obey you as your slave, as the slave of him who has the ring on his finger, both I and the other slaves of the ring."

"Pray, then, take me out of this place," said Aladdin, hardly knowing what was going on.

In a moment Aladdin found himself on the spot where the fire had been made. He felt the fresh breeze blow upon him, and, losing no time, made the best of his way home. How he ran, to be sure!

His mother was glad to see him, and, as she set him something to eat, he told her all about the strange cave and the lamp. He also showed her the precious stones which he had culled from the trees. Then he went to bed.

Next day he rose and asked for breakfast. Alas! there was no food in the house, for he had eaten it all the night before at supper. "If you will wait a little, my son," said his mother, "I will sell a little cotton which I have spun, and then I can buy some food."

"Nay," said Aladdin, "keep your cotton, Mother, and I will sell the lamp instead."

"It will fetch a better price if I clean it," said his mother, and with that she began to rub the lamp.

Before she could turn round, a genie stood before her. "What do you wish?" roared he with a voice like thunder. "I am ready to obey you as your slave, and the slave of those who have the lamp in their hands, both I and the other slaves of the lamp."

The mother could not speak, she was so full of fear. Aladdin, however, who had seen a genie before, and had good cause to be thankful, took the lamp from his mother's hands, and said in a firm voice, "I am hungry. Bring me something to eat."

In a moment the table was spread with all sorts of good things in dishes of gold and silver.

"What is the meaning of this?" said the good woman. "Has the Sultan taken pity on us and sent them?"

It took some time for Aladdin to explain to his mother all that he knew of the ring and the lamp. Being sore afraid, she would have nothing to do with such evil spirits, as she was sure they must be. "Ah, child." said she, "put the lamp away. I would rather you threw it away or sold it, than I would run the risk of ever touching it again."

"And I," said Aladdin, "will take care what I do with the things which have been so useful to me in times of trouble."

Enough food was left from breakfast to last for two days. When this was gone Aladdin went to sell one of the silver plates. He soon found a Jew who bought it, but gave him little for it. With the money some more food was bought. This went on for some time. As often as food was wanted a plate was sold, until there was only one large dish left.

Aladdin sold this at a better price, and with the money lived for a long time. He also bought fine clothes and rings to wear. In fact, he became quite a gentleman.

It chanced, one day, that Aladdin saw the princess, the daughter of the Sultan. Now Aladdin had never seen a lady's face before, except his mother's, for in that land all ladies go about with their faces hidden under a veil. This time the princess's face was unveiled.

"How I should like to marry the princess!" said Aladdin, almost aloud. "She is so pretty."

That same night Aladdin told his mother whom he had seen, and what had passed in his mind the moment he saw her. His mother told him not to be foolish. "Who can ask such a thing of the Sultan?" said she.

"You must ask yourself," replied Aladdin in a moment.

"I?" cried his mother, with surprise. "I go to

the Sultan? Not I, indeed. I will take care I do
not go on any such errand."

"But indeed you must, Mother; and, what is
more, you shall," said Aladdin, in a pet. "You
must not refuse me, or I shall die."

Thus Aladdin begged hard, but his mother
would not change her mind. "Think," said she,
"who you are. What have you ever done for your
prince? You can ask for no favour, I am sure.
And, besides, those who ask favours always give
presents. Tell me, what have you to give?"

For a moment or two Aladdin could make no
reply. Then he thought of the fruit which he had
brought from the cave, which, he had found out,
was of great value.

"The jewels, Mother," said he, "will make a
nice present for the Sultan."

Fetching the precious stones, he put them in
rows and groups on the table. They shone so
brightly that both mother and son were nearly
blinded. "Here is a rich present for the Sultan,"
said Aladdin. "Take them to him, and I am sure
you will get whatever you ask for."

"I cannot, my son," said his mother. "The
Sultan will order us both to be put to death."

"Nay, do not distress yourself, dear Mother,"
said Aladdin. "Has not the lamp been a friend to
us for these years past? and now I do not think
it will desert us. At all events, try; do, Mother
dear."

The good woman had now not a word to say,

and in a day or two was ready to try her luck at the palace.

She took a dish with the jewels in, and folded it up in a fine linen cloth. She then took another less fine, and tied the four corners of it, that she might carry it with ease. Then she set off for the palace.

The grand vizier and all the rest of the court had gone in when she came to the gate. There was a large crowd outside, but at last the gate was opened, and she went into the divan with the others. She then placed herself right in front of the Sultan.

When the court was over the Sultan went out, and the vizier and the rest went after. The people then had to go away. For several days this sort of thing took place, and each time Aladdin was sore vexed.

One day, when the court was over and the Sultan had gone to his own room, he said to his vizier, "For some time past I have seen a woman, who has come every day I hold my court, and who carries something in her hand tied up in a linen cloth. She puts herself in front of me. Do you know what she wants?"

The vizier did not wish the Sultan to think he had not seen her. So he said, "Oh, she seems to have come on a small errand. Some one has been selling her some bad meat."

This did not please the Sultan, for he did not think that could be the reason for a woman coming to him every day as this one had done. "The very next day the court sits," said he to the vizier, "if this woman comes, do not fail to call her, that I may hear what she has to say."

The vizier then kissed the Sultan's hand, and placed it on his head to show that he would sooner die than not do his duty.

It had now become no trouble for Aladdin's mother to go to the court, as she was quite used to it. The next time the court met, there she was, right in front of the Sultan.

The vizier pointed to her, which was the order for her to go to the throne and make known her wants.

Aladdin's mother bowed and took up her place. The Sultan then spoke to her in these words: "My good woman, for a long time past I have seen you at the court, but no one has spoken to you. What is your request?"

"I dare not tell you in the open court, in front of all these people," said the woman.

"Then have the court cleared," said the Sultan to the vizier. "This woman shall tell us what she wants in secret."

"Now, my good woman," said the Sultan, when all had gone out, "what do you want?"

"I am afraid even now to make it known, for you may put me to death for my pains," said Aladdin's mother.

"Whatever it may be," said the Sultan, "I pardon you from this moment; not the least harm shall come to you from anything you may say. Be bold, and speak out."

Aladdin's mother then told the Sultan how her son had seen the princess, and wished to make her his wife. He was not in the least angry, for he had given the woman full leave to say all she wished. Before he made any reply, he pointed to her bundle, and said, "What have you there, tied up so well?"

At once the woman opened her bundle and gave the jewels to the Sultan. "They are a present for your highness," said she. "They come from my son."

The Sultan could not speak for a moment; the jewels were so rich and rare he had never before seen any so fine. Then he looked at them one by one. "How grand!" said he. "What say you, vizier, to such a present?"

"They are, in truth, of great value," said the vizier.

"Ay, indeed," said the Sultan. "Must not he who sends such a present be worthy of the princess my daughter, and must I not give her to him who comes and asks for her at such a price?"

Now, some time before this took place, the Sultan had told the vizier that he would bestow the hand of the princess on his son. The vizier was afraid, therefore, that the promise would be overlooked, and that after all his son would never be the Sultan's son-in-law, a thing upon which he had set his mind.

So the vizier stepped up to the Sultan and spoke something softly in his ear.

The Sultan started. Then, turning towards Aladdin's mother, he said to her, "Go, my good woman, return to your home, and tell your son that I cannot give my daughter to him for three months. At the end of that time you must return here."

Aladdin's mother went from the court with all speed and made quick steps for home. There she met her son, who had been awaiting her return. "What news, Mother?" asked he.

Now Aladdin saw quite clearly that his mother's visit to the Sultan had not been in vain this time: for, in the first place, she was back long before he thought she would come ; and, in the second, she looked very pleased. He thought it would give his mother joy, however, to ask her.

When she had taken off her veil, and had sat down on the sofa by his side, she said, "My son, I will tell you first that you need not give up all hope of being the Sultan's son-in-law. I gave the Sultan your present, and, though he was quite taken by surprise at the request I made to him, he was not displeased. At the end of three months I am to go to the court again, when the Sultan will tell me what he has made up his mind to do."

Aladdin thought himself the most happy of men. He jumped and danced about for joy, and kissed his mother over and over again. He called her a good woman, and told her what a grand lady he would make her when he should be wedded to the princess.

The three months went by very slowly indeed. To Aladdin they seemed to be an age, but at last they were over. Aladdin did not fail to send his mother to the palace on the very next morning, to put the Sultan in mind of his promise.

She went, therefore, to the palace, as her son wished, and took up her place near the Sultan. The Sultan no sooner cast his eyes that way than he knew her face, and called to mind the strange request she had made and the exact time to which he had put it off.

The Sultan called his vizier. " I see there," said he, "that good woman who brought me the jewels three months ago. Bid her come forward, and we will hear what she has to say."

The vizier doing as he was told, called the woman, who threw herself on the ground at the foot of the throne.

After she had risen the Sultan asked what she wished. "Sire," said she, "I have come to remind you of your promise to my son. The three months have gone by. What may I tell him when I return home? "

Now when the Sultan put the woman off for three months, he thought he should never see or hear from her again, since he knew how foolish the request was. Turning to his vizier, he asked him what he should now do.

"Sire," said the vizier, "it seems to be a very

strange request, but it can be refused in an easy way without giving offence to any one. Set a very high price upon the princess your daughter, so that all his riches, however great they may be, cannot reach the value. That will be the way to put a stop to his requests."

The Sultan agreed, and in a few moments said to Aladdin's mother: "Sultans, my good woman, ought always to keep their words, and I am ready to hold mine; but, as I cannot give my daughter to any one unless I know him to be a rich man, tell your son I will keep my word as soon as he shall send me forty large basins of pure gold quite full of the same sort of things which you have already given to me. The basins must be brought each by a black slave, led by a white slave, young, well made, and richly dressed. These are the terms. Go, tell them to your son."

Aladdin's mother once more fell at the Sultan's feet, and then withdrew from the court. On her way home she smiled within herself at the foolish thoughts of her son. "Where, indeed," said she, "is he to find so many gold basins and such a lot of jewels to fill them? Will he go back to the cave, the entrance to which is shut up, in order to gather them from the trees? And where can he get all those handsome slaves whom the Sultan demands?"

As she went into the house her mind was full of these thoughts, and, meeting her son, she said, "All hope is lost, my son; think no more of the princess. The Sultan did, indeed, treat me with kindness, but I do not suppose for a moment that you will be able to meet his demands."

She then told him all that the vizier had said, adding, "He is even now waiting for your reply; but, between ourselves, he may wait a long time."

"Not so long as you may think, my dear mother," said Aladdin. "I will give the Sultan a great surprise. While I am thinking what to do, go and get dinner and leave me to myself."

As soon as his mother had gone out to buy the dinner, Aladdin took the lamp, and, having rubbed it, the genie stood before him.

In a gentle voice—for this time Aladdin had rubbed the lamp more gently than before—the genie asked the same question: "What do you wish? I am ready to obey you as your slave, and the slave of those who have the lamp in their hands, both I and the other slaves of the lamp."

Aladdin lost no time in telling the genie what he wanted. "The Sultan," said he, "agrees to give me the hand of the princess his daughter in marriage, but he first demands forty large basins of gold filled to the very top with that fruit of the garden from which I took the lamp that you are the slave of. He asks also that these forty basins shall be carried by as many black slaves, each led by a young and handsome white slave in rich attire. Go; get me his present as soon as you can, that I may send it to the Sultan before the court is over."

The genie said that it should be done at once. In a very short time he came back, bringing with him the slaves and the basins full of jewels. Each basin was covered with a cloth of silver, and the slaves were richly dressed. There were so many of them that they filled the house, as well as the court in front and the garden behind.

The genie asked Aladdin if there were any further orders for him; and on being told no, went quickly out of sight.

Aladdin's mother now coming back from the market was in the greatest surprise to see so many persons and so much riches. Having set down the food which she had brought with her, she was about to take off her veil, but Aladdin put his hand on her shoulder and stopped her.

"My dear mother," cried he, "there is no time to lose. Go with these to the court at once, and tell the Sultan they are for him."

Without waiting for her reply, Aladdin opened the door that led into the street, and told all the slaves to go out one after the other. He then put a white slave in front of each of the black ones, who carried the golden basins on their heads.

When his mother, who went with the last black slave, had gone out, he shut the door, and waited quietly in his room, thinking that now the Sultan would be sure to give him his daughter for a wife.

Every one in the street stopped to see the long line of eighty slaves. The dress of each slave was made of a rich stuff, and so covered with precious stones that those who were good judges thought each of them worth more than a kingdom.

The graceful manner of each slave caused those who saw them not to take their eyes from them, so that each person stood in the same place in the street where he was.

As the way was long it took some time to get to the palace gates, but at last they were reached.

When the first of the eighty slaves was about to pass through, the porters took him to be a king, so richly was he dressed. They were about to kiss the hem of his robe when the slave, who had had his orders from the genie, stopped them, saying, "Our master will come when the time shall be proper."

Through the gates the slaves all went one after the other, and soon found their way into the court. Their dresses were far more splendid than those of the Sultan's officers, or even the Sultan's. The slaves made two rows and stood on two sides in front of the throne.

The mother of Aladdin then threw herself at the Sultan's feet, and when she had been told to rise, said, "This, sire, is what my son sends in answer to your demands. He awaits your reply."

The Sultan hardly heard the good woman speak, for he could not take his eyes away from the slaves and the golden basins of jewels which they had brought.

At length he turned to the vizier, and, in a loud voice, so that all might hear, said, "Well, vizier, what think you of the person, whoever he may be, who has now sent me so rich and fine a present, a person whom neither of us knows or has heard of before? Do you not think he is worthy of the princess my daughter?"

It was the duty of the vizier to make a reply that would please the Sultan, so he answered, "Far be it from me, sire, to say nay to such a person who can send a present like this."

Then all the people in the court clapped their hands in glee, and the Sultan rose from his throne. "Go, my good woman," said he, "and tell your son that I am waiting with open arms to embrace him. The sooner he comes to claim the hand of the princess my daughter, the more pleased I shall be."

Aladdin's mother bowed and retired. The Sultan then sent everybody away but the vizier. He told the slaves to carry the golden basins and the jewels into the palace that he might show them to the Sultana and his daughter.

In the meantime, Aladdin's mother, reaching home, showed by her manner how she had got on with the Sultan. Nor did she lose a moment in telling her son what had taken place. "The Sultan awaits you," added she, "and I advise you to make yourself fit to appear before him."

Aladdin went to his own room and took down the lamp which had been so true a friend to him.

No sooner had he rubbed it than the genie again showed himself ready to do his bidding.

"Genie," said Aladdin, "I want you to take me to the bath, and when I have bathed, to have a rich and handsome dress ready for me."

Aladdin had no sooner given his orders than he was lifted up and carried through the air without being seen. Then he was put into a bath of the finest marble, where he was washed and rubbed with sweet perfumes. His skin became white and fresh, and his body felt lighter and more active.

He then went to the dressing-room, where, in place of his old robe, he found one more rich and handsome than a Sultan's. By the help of the genie, who waited on him, he put on each part until he was quite dressed.

Then the genie took him home in the same way as he had carried him to the bath. "Have you any further demands?" he asked.

"Yes," said Aladdin. "Bring me a horse as soon as you can, which shall be more beautiful than any horse in the Sultan's stables, and let the saddle and bridle and the trappings be worth more than a million pounds. Let them flash with jewels of all kinds.

"I order you also at the same time to get me twenty slaves as well and richly dressed as those who carried the basins of gold, to walk on each side and behind me, and twenty more to walk in two ranks before me. You must also get six female slaves to wait on my mother. These must be dressed more richly than the princess. I also want ten thousand pieces of gold in ten purses. These are all my commands at present. Go, and make all haste."

All in a moment the genie went and came back. He brought the horse, the slaves, ten of whom had each a purse with ten thousand pieces of gold in every one, and the six female slaves each with a fine dress for Aladdin's mother wrapped in a piece of silver cloth. These he gave to Aladdin.

Aladdin took only four of the ten purses, and gave them to his mother, as he said she might want them. He left the other six in the hands of the slaves, and told them that as they went along the streets they were to throw the coins in heaps to the people.

He then gave the six female slaves to his mother, telling her that they were for her, and that the dresses which they had in the silver cloths were for her use.

And now a start was made for the palace. Aladdin mounted his horse and began the march in the order we have told. Though he had never been on horseback in his life he rode quite well, and everybody praised the grace he showed in the saddle.

The streets were thronged with people, who shouted and cheered as the slaves threw the gold pieces among them. Aladdin was so changed in looks and dress that no one knew him, not even those with whom he had played in the streets.

This all came from the power of the wonderful lamp.

At length the palace was reached. The Sultan was overjoyed to see so handsome a man as Aladdin, and so gay and rich a dress as he wore. He himself had not one so thickly covered with jewels. He came down from his throne two or three steps so as to prevent Aladdin from falling down at his feet, and holding out his hand, put Aladdin to sit between himself and the vizier.

Aladdin then rose and spoke to the Sultan in these words: "O sire, I beg you not to think me rash in asking for the hand of the princess your daughter, but I should die if I did not have her for my wife."

The Sultan was charmed with Aladdin, and made a sign. At once the air was filled with the sounds of trumpets and cymbals, and Aladdin was led by the Sultan into a saloon where a great feast was served up. The Sultan and Aladdin sat at a table together and the vizier and the chief guards waited on them.

The Sultan talked as a friend with Aladdin, and was more and more pleased with him each moment. Then he gave orders for the marriage papers to be made ready.

Aladdin, however, did not wish the wedding to take place at once. He told the Sultan that first of all he wanted to prepare a house, good and large, fit for a princess.

"That is well," said the Sultan. "There is a

large open space before my palace. Take that, and build a house upon it fit for my daughter the princess."

Then Aladdin, going home, called the genie, to whom he gave orders to build him a house on the space of ground in front of the palace. It was to be built of precious stones and to contain a room full of gold for his use.

Knowing the house would be built to his orders, Aladdin sent his mother, richly dressed and attended by her slaves, to tell the princess it was ready. She set out at once.

That same night the house was built. It rose in the air with its rooms one above another. Its walls shone and its furniture was of pure gold and pearls.

In the morning the porters opened the gates of the palace, and were not able to believe their eyes, for, till that moment, they had never seen so large and so handsome a building as that which they now saw. The Sultan saw it, and called his vizier who put it down to magic. "We shall see," he said, "what is to come of all this finery of Aladdin's."

And now the marriage took place. Nothing like it had been seen in all the world before. There were gold and silver dishes and cups, wines of the rarest sorts, and cakes of the best.

For some time Aladdin and the princess lived in happiness. They loved each other dearly, and were a joy to the Sultan and the Sultana. Sad to say, an event took place which put an end to it all.

The magician had been away from China, but now he began to think of the lamp and what had become of it. By his magic he found out it was still Aladdin's, and that he had become a rich man and a prince. The magician once more went to the city. There he saw the fine house which Aladdin had built, and felt pretty sure that the lamp was somewhere inside. Oh, if he could only tell where!

He thought of a plan. He went to the shop of a man who made and sold lamps. "I want," said he to the man, " a dozen copper lamps. Can you make them for me?"

"To be sure!" replied the man. "You may have them to-morrow."

Next day the magician had the lamps sent to his inn, and he thereupon took them round the city in a basket crying out, "Who will change old lamps for new?"

Everybody thought the magician was mad, and laughed at him. "That man," said they, "has surely lost his senses to offer new lamps for old ones." And the children hooted after him as he went along.

By-and-by he came to the street which led to Aladdin's house and the Sultan's palace. Aladdin had gone to the hunt, but his princess sat at an open window at her spinning with her maidens. All of them heard the cry, "Who will change old lamps for new ones?"

One of the maidens laughed at the idea of changing old lamps for new, and said that the man must be joking. Then it was agreed to try him with Aladdin's lamp. "Take it down," said the princess; "we shall then see if he is a madman or not."

Now Aladdin had never spoken of the lamp to his wife, nor had she the least idea that it was through the lamp that so much wealth and honour had come to her husband.

The slave went down to the street with the lamp, which the magician saw and knew in a moment. "A new lamp for an old one?" said he. "Ay, truly," said the slave; "the princess desires it." The slave then chose out a pretty new lamp, leaving the old one with the magician, and ran off to her mistress.

No sooner did the magician get the lamp in his hands than he went back towards his inn. On the way he passed along a very quiet street, where he put down his basket of new lamps and left them. Then, instead of going to his inn, he turned through the gate of the city and got out into the country.

When night came on he drew the lamp from his bosom and rubbed it. "What do you wish?" cried the genie, who had come in an instant. "I am ready to obey you as your slave, and the slave of those who have the lamp in their hands, both I and the other slaves of the lamp."

"I command you to take up the house, which

you and the other slaves of the lamp have built, near the Sultan's palace, and carry it with me and all that is in it, dead and alive, to Africa," said the magician.

At once he and the whole palace was lifted up and carried by the genie right to the spot where the magician desired.

Next day, as soon as it was light, the Sultan cast his eyes towards the palace of Aladdin. Alas! there was nothing left but the open space of land on which it had been built. He thought his eyes were grown dim, and that he could not see; so he rubbed them. Still there was no Aladdin's palace. Then he called his vizier. "Look there," cried he. "The new palace is gone. It has not fallen, or the ruins would be left. Alas! my poor daughter is gone. Where is the wretch who asked her for a wife? I will strike off his head."

The Sultan was told that Aladdin had been gone to the hunt these two days. "Then send thirty of my horsemen to drag him before me in chains."

The horsemen were at once sent into the forest where Aladdin had gone, and there they found him. "Prince Aladdin," said the chief of the horsemen, "I am sorry to have to tell you that you must come to the Sultan. I hope you will pardon me, but I must do my duty."

He then took hold of Aladdin, bound him hand and foot, and carried him to the Sultan.

The moment the Sultan saw him he ordered his head to be struck off.

"Not so fast, sire," put in the vizier. "Do you not see the people making their way into the palace? Aladdin has been kind to them, and they are now going to shield him from your wrath and save him."

The Sultan looked, and saw a huge crowd of people, with swords drawn, coming with all speed to the palace. His face showed that he was in great fear. "Put up your sword," said he to the headsman, "and you, vizier, tell the people that Aladdin is safe from harm. I pardon him."

This was done.

When all was quiet the Sultan called Aladdin to him. "What have I done, sire, to vex you?" asked Aladdin, who had not yet been told what had taken place.

"Don't talk to me," said the Sultan. "Where is my dear daughter? Where is the house you built for her on the open space in front of my palace? Where? I say. Where?"

Aladdin looked through the window of the room he was in, and lo! he too was struck dumb for a moment. "Sire," said he, "the palace is surely gone, but I have had no hand in it. Pray give me forty days in which to search for your daughter, my wife; and if I do not find her, you may kill me."

This was granted, and Aladdin left the Sultan to mourn alone. Going through the city, he asked all he met if they had seen anything done to his palace, whereupon they thought he had gone mad. Then he made up his mind to leave the city and make his search beyond it.

Towards night he found himself near a river, and the idea came to him that he would drown himself. But, as he stepped down the steep bank he slipped, and in doing so rubbed the ring he was wearing on the rock.

"What do you wish?" cried the genie, who had come in an instant. "I am ready to obey you as your slave, and the slave of him who has the ring upon his finger, both I and the other slaves of the ring."

How strange that Aladdin should not have thought of the ring before! "Welcome, dear genie," cried he. "Thou hast saved my life before. Save it again by giving me back my palace and my dear wife, the princess."

"What you ask," said the genie, "is not in my power. I am only the slave of the ring; you must address yourself to the slave of the lamp."

"In that case, then," said Aladdin, "at least take me to the spot where my palace is, and place me under the window of the princess." He had barely said this before the genie, lifting him up, bore him through the air to Africa, near a large city, and in the midst of a meadow, in which the palace stood. Setting him down under one of the windows of the princess's room, he there left him.

All this was the work of an instant.

It was night, and Aladdin slept soundly beneath a tree. Next morning he was roused by the

princess opening the window. He looked up and
there saw her. She saw him too, and bade him
come to her through a secret door.

Soon they embraced each other with tears of
joy, and then Aladdin asked her what had become
of the lamp. The poor princess told him all, and
begged him to forgive her, which he did, saying
it must be got again by some means. He felt sure
that the taking away of the palace was the work
of the magician.

Then Aladdin formed his plans. He went into
the city and bought a drug, which he gave to the
princess later in the day, asking her to put it in
the magician's wine at supper that evening.

The princess hardly liked to do such a thing,
even though the magician had treated her so ill;
but she did it, and no sooner had he drunk his
wine than he sank a helpless corpse on the floor.

Aladdin lay in hiding near the palace, and at a
signal went to the princess. All the slaves and
servants were sent to their own rooms while
Aladdin searched for the lamp. He found it in
the magician's bosom, and at once rubbed it
hard.

In less time than it takes to tell the story the
genie came, to whom Aladdin gave orders for the
palace to be carried back just as it was to China.

The Sultan, who, in the meantime, had hardly
had a wink of sleep, looked once more through
his window and beheld the palace in its place.
Aladdin, who had risen early, thought the Sultan

would lose no time in coming to see his daughter, so he went out to meet him. The Sultan came, and he and Aladdin were friends once more. Great was the joy of every one of them, and all trouble was cast aside.

Now it chanced that the magician had a brother from whom he had been parted many years. This brother found out that the magician had been put to death by poison, and that it had been done by a princess who was wedded to a rich man of low birth. He looked for this princess in all parts of the world, and at last came to the city where Aladdin lived.

In the city there also lived a holy woman whose name was Fatima. The magician's brother made his way to her, and bade her, under pain of death, to change her clothes for his. When this was done the brother, whom we will now call Fatima and speak of as a woman, went to the palace of Aladdin and began to talk with the princess.

So pleased was the princess with the holy woman that she asked her to stay with her in the palace.

That was just what Fatima wanted, so she said she would. "Rise, then," said the princess, "follow me, and we will choose your room."

Fatima did so with feeble steps, and soon the holy woman was lodged in the palace. Every day she saw the princess, and the two became fast friends.

One day, when walking through the rooms,

they came to the saloon which was the best room in the palace. Fatima said she liked it very much, but there was one thing wanting—the egg of a roc hung from the centre dome.

When Aladdin came home, having been absent for some days, the princess was sad. "What is the matter, my dear?" he asked. "Have you not all you wish for to make you happy?"

"I thought we had the most beautiful palace in the world," said the princess, "but now I find out that there is one thing wanting to make it complete—the egg of a roc hung from the centre dome of the saloon."

"As for that," said Aladdin, "it shall be done at once." Then going to the saloon he rubbed the lamp, which he now always kept in his bosom. The genie came, and, on hearing what Aladdin wished, he gave such a wild and loud shriek that the walls of all the palace shook.

"Wretch," cried the genie, "you want me to hang my master from the dome; but it is a good thing for you that the request is not your own. It comes from the magician's brother, who is now in this palace, dressed as a holy woman. Find him, and slay him at once."

Then Aladdin went back to the princess, and the holy woman was sent for. She came, and Aladdin asked her to cure a pain which he had in his head.

Now was the holy woman's chance to slay Aladdin and secure the lamp.

He bent his head for Fatima to place her hand

upon it, when lo! all at once Aladdin rose, seized a dagger which Fatima had already grasped from under her cloak, and thrust it into her heart.

"What have you done?" cried the princess.

"This is not a holy woman at all," said Aladdin, "but the brother of that cruel magician who has done us both so much hurt. He has come to his fate. Now we shall indeed be happy."

These words were spoken in truth, for Aladdin and his dear princess lived for many years in each other's love; and, when the Sultan died, Aladdin took his place and ruled his land in peace.

THE STORY OF ABOU-HASSAN THE WAG,
OR THE SLEEPER AWAKENED

WHEN the Caliph Haroun al Raschid was king, there lived at Bagdad a merchant who had one son called Abou-Hassan the Wag. His father, wishing very much that this son should grow up to be a wise and clever man, was always teaching him something. He would make the little boy stand before him, and with lifted finger ask him many questions. There was always a cane hidden behind his father's back, and if Abou-Hassan could not answer these questions, it would come down sharply on his shoulders.

But while Abou-Hassan was still very young, his father died, and left him great riches. He divided these into two parts—half to save, and half to spend; and, as he had a great many friends who were all fond of spending money, half of his riches was soon all gone.

When Abou-Hassan found he had no money left to spend, he told his friends; but they did not care, as they had only liked him because he was rich, and shared all he had with them. This made him sad, and he told his mother, who tried to comfort him, for she knew they were not real friends who did not care for him now that he was poor.

Saying farewell to these untrue friends, Abou-Hassan began to live very carefully upon the other half of his riches. He made up his mind that he would talk only to strangers, and that he would have a new friend every night. So when night came he always sat on the bridge, and invited a passing stranger to go home with him to supper. When morning came he sent his guest away, and never spoke to him again; and this he did every night for a year.

One day, when he was sitting on the bridge as usual, the Caliph and some of his servants passed by. Abou-Hassan did not know it was the Caliph, because he was dressed like an ordinary man, having come out to walk about the streets just like any one else. So, catching hold of him, he said, "Oh, my master, come home and feast with me."

"Lead the way," replied the Caliph, and he followed the young man to his house, which he was surprised to find was such a fine one. Its walls were covered with wonderful things, and in the middle played a fountain which looked like dancing gold.

"Tell me all about yourself," said the Caliph, "that I may reward you for your kindness."

"Alas!" answered Abou-Hassan, "we cannot be friends. I shall see you no more after to-night."

"Why so?" asked the Caliph, who, when Abou-

Hassan had told him all the story of his untrue friends, said he did not wonder that the young man was afraid of making new ones.

The feast being over, the Caliph asked Abou-Hassan if he had any great wish. And Abou-Hassan said his greatest wish was to punish the sheikhs who lived at the nearest mosque. They were the priests, and whenever they heard music and noise in Abou-Hassan's house, they would send the judge to punish him and make him pay fines.

"May you have your wish," said the Caliph, and when Abou-Hassan was not looking, put something into his cup which made him go to sleep. As soon as he was fast asleep, the Caliph called his servants, and they carried Abou-Hassan away to the Caliph's palace, and put him in the royal bed.

Then the Caliph, calling together his chief servants, told them that when Abou-Hassan awoke they were to pretend he was the Caliph, and do everything that he told them. And the real Caliph went away and hid himself.

When Abou-Hassan awoke in the morning he was surprised to find himself in a palace, with servants kneeling beside his bed and kissing the ground before him.

"Oh, our lord, it is the time for morning prayer," said one of them; and Abou-Hassan laughed, because he did not know himself. He looked at the walls of blue and gold, the silken curtains and golden cups, the lighted lamps and

many slaves and thought he must be dreaming.
He called a slave, and said, "Tell me where I am
and who I am."

"Oh, Prince of the Faithful, you are the Caliph
of the country," replied the slave, bowing very
low.

"You are telling lies," said Abou-Hassan
angrily; but on the other slaves drawing near and
telling him he was indeed the Caliph, he began to
believe it himself.

"Yesterday I was Abou-Hassan: to-day I am the
Caliph. Whatever has happened to me?" he said
to himself, as the slaves began to dress him. One
brought him gold shoes trimmed with rubies, and
Abou-Hassan was afraid to put them on. He
washed his hands in a golden basin, and then the
slaves brought him a splendid robe.

"I am sure the wicked fairies have done it all,"
he said; but as soon as he was dressed, a slave came
to ask if he had any commands that must be
obeyed in the city.

"Yes," cried Abou-Hassan, thinking this a fine
chance to punish his enemies. "I command that
the four sheikhs in the nearest mosque have each a
thousand blows. And when that is done, let a
paper be written to say that they must live no
longer in the street where the mosque is. Also
mount them upon mules, with their faces towards
the animals' tails, and take them round the city,
calling out that this is the punishment of those
who trouble their neighbours."

"It shall be done, oh prince," said the slaves humbly. "Have you no other commands?"

"Yes! I have one more," said Abou-Hassan again. "Go to a little street near the mosque, and ask for the house of Abou-Hassan the Wag. Give his mother a hundred pieces of gold from me."

"Yes, oh prince," answered all the slaves.

"Now you may depart," ordered Abou-Hassan, for he was beginning to feel quite like a real Caliph.

When the slaves had gone, he called for something to eat, and was taken to another splendid room, where a table covered with good things was waiting.

"It must have been the king of the genii who had supper with me last night," he said to himself. "This is his way of rewarding me, and I am now among the fairies."

While he was thus talking to himself, one of the slave girls filled his cup with wine. He did not see what she was doing, and she put into it something that sent him to sleep again.

The real Caliph then coming out of his hiding-place, told the slaves to carry Abou-Hassan to his own home once more, and to lay him on his own bed, which they did. And when he awoke to find it quite dark, he called out to know where he was. But nobody answered him, until his mother, hearing him shouting, ran to see what was the matter.

"Who are you, old woman?" he asked, when he

saw her, for he still thought he was in the Caliph's palace.

"I am your mother," she answered, feeling rather afraid.

"You are not," shouted Abou-Hassan. "Do you not know that I am the Caliph, and lord of the country and the people?"

"Oh! do be quiet," said the old mother. "If any one hears you say such things, you will be put into prison. Listen to me, for I have good news for you. Yesterday the Caliph ordered your enemies to be sent away, and he sent me a hundred gold pieces as a present."

Abou-Hassan gave a great cry when he heard this, and said, "It was *I* who sent you the gold, and *I* am the Prince of the Faithful." He seized a stick and beat his old mother because she would not believe him, until the neighbours rushed in and stopped him.

"This man is mad," they all shouted, and tying his hands behind his back, carried him off to a place where they shut him up by himself. They put a chain round his neck and fastened it to a heavy door, and every day gave him a good beating and some very nasty medicine.

When he had been there ten days, his mother came to visit him. She looked in at him through the window, and saw him sitting very quietly, for Abou-Hassan had now time to think, and he began to feel sure he had only dreamed that he was the Caliph.

On seeing his mother, he told her he was sorry that he had beaten her and done such strange things, and she forgave him, and took him home with her again.

Every one could see that he was cured of his madness, but soon growing tired of living quietly alone, he went out one day to sit on the bridge. And as he sat there, the Caliph came along, this time dressed as a merchant.

"Do not come near me, king of the wicked genii," cried Abou-Hassan. "It was you who made me think I was the Caliph, and caused me to be shut up as a madman, and I will not have you for my companion."

"Why! what have I done?" asked the Caliph, with a laugh.

"As much as you could to hurt me," said Abou-Hassan, who told the Caliph all the story of his troubles.

"Well," said the Caliph, "I did one kind action for you: I helped you to get rid of your enemies, the sheikhs."

"Yes," replied Abou-Hassan slowly, "you did that," and he began to feel less angry with the Caliph. In fact, before very long they became friends, and Abou-Hassan went to live at the palace, and became the greatest favourite of the Caliph and of his wife, the lady Zobeide.

After a time he married one of Zobeide's maidens, whose name was Nouzatalfuad. She was very beautiful, and they lived happily together for a long time. But, being both fond of spending money, they found out one day that they had spent every piece of gold they possessed, and had nothing left.

Abou-Hassan sat down to wonder how he could get some more, and remembering that the Caliph had once played a trick upon him, resolved to play a trick upon the Caliph.

So he said to his wife, "We will pretend to be dead. I will lie down and you must spread a silk cover over me, and then tell the lady Zobeide. You must cry and scream, and she will be very sorry for you, and will give you two hundred gold pieces and two pieces of silk. Then you must pretend to be dead, and I will go and tell the Caliph, and he will give me the same."

Abou-Hassan and his wife then carried out this plan. Zobeide wept when she heard that Abou-Hassan the Wag was dead, and gave his wife the gold and the silk. The Caliph too was very sorry to hear that Abou-Hassan had lost his beautiful wife, and gave him a piece of silk and two hundred pieces of gold to pay for her funeral.

Abou-Hassan was so pleased with the success of his plan that he danced about the room, though every one thought he was dead, and he and his wife had quite a big heap of gold pieces between them. They spread out their pieces of silk, and admired them very much, and sat laughing together for a long time.

Now soon after Abou-Hassan had told him of

the death of his wife, the Caliph went to tell
Zobeide how sorry he was that she had lost her
favourite maiden. His chief slave, Mesrour, went
with him, but, on reaching Zobeide's room, they
found her waiting to tell the Caliph how grieved
she was to hear *his* friend Abou-Hassan was dead.

The Caliph smiled, and said to Mesrour,
"Women have no sense. It is not Abou-Hassan
who is dead; it is his beautiful wife."

"No! no!" cried the lady Zobeide. "Nouzatalfuad is alive and well, but she came to me in great
grief not long ago, to tell me that Abou-Hassan
is dead."

"This is nonsense," said the Caliph. "It is
Nouzatalfuad who is dead."

"Indeed, my lord," cried Zobeide again, "I am
sure it is Abou-Hassan."

The Caliph now grew angry, though not quite
sure in his own mind whom to be angry with. He
looked very fierce, as all the members of his family
did when they were angry, and called out to
Mesrour, saying, "Go at once to the house of
Abou-Hassan and see who is really dead."

Mesrour, setting off as fast as he could go, ran
all the way. On reaching the little street where
Abou-Hassan lived, he saw him looking out of the
window, and Abou-Hassan saw Mesrour coming.

"Here is Mesrour," he said to his wife. "I
expect the Caliph has sent him to see which of us
is dead. You must pretend to be dead when he
comes in, and then the Caliph will believe me."

So, as Nouzatalfuad lay down and kept very still, Mesrour thought he saw the maiden lying dead. Being quite sure that Abou-Hassan had told the truth, he went home again to tell the Caliph, and Abou-Hassan, peeping out of the curtains, laughed at him as he hurried along with his big stick.

When he got back to the palace, he knelt at the Caliph's feet, and said, "Oh, my lord, it is indeed Nouzatalfuad who is dead, for I saw her lying there with my own eyes, and Abou-Hassan is full of grief."

When the lady Zobeide heard what Mesrour said, it was her turn to be angry.

"Why do you believe what that slave says?" she cried. "I shall send someone myself to see whether Abou-Hassan is not dead, for I am sure that he is." She called an old woman who always spoke the truth, and giving her some money, told her to find out what had really happened.

The old woman ran as fast as she could, but Abou-Hassan saw her coming. "Here is a messenger from the lady Zobeide," he said. "Now *I* will pretend to be dead, so that she will believe *you*."

So Abou-Hassan lay still, and when the old woman reached the house, she was met by Nouzatalfuad.

"See what has happened to me: Abou-Hassan is dead," she screamed, "and I am left alone in the world. Oh! how good he was to me."

"I am sorry for you," said the old woman. "And now I will go back and tell my mistress the truth, for Mesrour declares that Abou-Hassan is alive, and you are dead."

"Why, I told my mistress that I had lost my good husband," cried Nouzatalfuad, pretending to be surprised. "And she gave me two hundred pieces of gold and some rich silk. I wish that I had really died, and he had lived. Whatever shall I do without him?" And she and the old woman wept together.

When the old woman, returning to the palace, told this story, Zobeide was quite sure that Mesrour had been telling lies. Sending for him, she told him what the old woman had said, and made him promise to tell the Caliph.

But Mesrour only said, "It is this old woman who tells lies. For I saw Abou-Hassan alive and well with my own eyes, and his wife lying dead."

This made the old woman very angry. "You know you are saying what is not true," she cried, "because you want to make everybody quarrel."

"Nothing of the kind," answered Mesrour. "The lady Zobeide believes you because she knows no better."

The lady Zobeide, getting into a great rage, told the Caliph what his slave had said, in a loud and angry voice. But the Caliph was so puzzled that he did not know what to believe.

"It seems as if I tell lies, and you tell lies, and Mesrour tells lies, and the old woman tells lies," he said to Zobeide. "And I think the best way to find out the truth is for us all to go together to the house of Abou-Hassan, and see who has spoken the truth."

So they all four arose and set out together to the little street where Abou-Hassan lived. The Caliph was quite sure it would now be proved that his friend was not dead, and Zobeide rejoiced to think that every one would soon know Mesrour to be untruthful.

But Abou-Hassan kept a strict watch from his window that day, for he wondered if any one else would come from the palace. And he saw the Caliph and Zobeide and the old woman and Mesrour coming quickly up the street.

"You may drop a jar without breaking it, which means that the time has come to be careful," he said to his wife, as she sat looking at him in horror and saying, "What *shall* we do?"

"Never fear," said Abou-Hassan calmly. "We will now *both* pretend to be dead." He lay down upon the low couch, and his wife lay by his side. They both closed their eyes, and covered themselves with a veil and then kept very still. Presently in walked the Caliph, the lady Zobeide, Mesrour the slave, and the old woman. They all stood in a row, and looked down upon Abou-Hassan and his wife, and said nothing, until Zobeide began to cry.

"Alas! alas!" she said. "They are *both* dead. I know how it is. My dear, beautiful maiden has mourned for her husband so much that she has died too."

"Do not be so foolish," said the Caliph. "Have I not told you that Abou-Hassan came to me tearing his clothes with grief because he had lost his beautiful wife? Did I not give him two hundred pieces of gold to pay for her funeral? Of course it is he who died last, because he could not live alone."

But Zobeide would not believe this, and she and the Caliph talked so long about it that at last he lost his patience.

Sitting down beside the couch where Abou-Hassan and his wife lay, he said in a loud voice, "If any one will tell me truly which of these two died first, I will give him a thousand pieces of gold."

Abou-Hassan no sooner heard these words than he sat straight up, though he was supposed to be dead.

"It was *I* who died first, oh Prince of the faithful," he said. "Please give me the thousand gold pieces that you have just promised to any one who will tell you the truth."

When she heard her husband say this, Nouzatalfuad sat up too, and told her lady Zobeide that she was not dead either, but that they had both been pretending. Zobeide was rather angry at the trick which they had played, but the Caliph did nothing but laugh. In fact, he laughed so much that he could hardly stand or speak, though he kept trying to tell Abou-Hassan what a funny man he was.

"Why did you not *ask* us for some money?" said the lady Zobeide.

"I was ashamed to do so," answered Nouzatalfuad.

"And I did not like to ask the Caliph for more, when I had spent all mine," added Abou-Hassan. "I had enough when I was alone, but since I married this maiden, I have spent a great deal more. In fact, I am quite sure I should spend it, however much I had, so please give me the thousand pieces you promised."

The Caliph and the lady Zobeide both laughed again, and as soon as they got back to the palace a thousand pieces of gold were given to Abou-Hassan. The Caliph was very glad that his friend was not dead, and from that day gave him enough money to live on every year. The lady Zobeide also gave a thousand pieces of gold to his wife, and Abou-Hassan and Nouzatalfuad lived together, and served the Caliph very happily, for a long, long time.

THE STORY OF THE FISHERMAN

THERE once lived a very old fisherman who was very poor. Every morning he went out to his work, but would never cast his net into the sea more than four times. This was one of the rules of his life.

One morning, while yet the moon was up, he cast in his net, and as he drew it out he said, "How heavy it is! I must surely have a fine catch of fish this time."

Alas! all that was in the net was the dead body of an ass. The fisherman at once threw it into the sea, and again cast in his net.

He found it hard to draw to land this time also, but there were no fish, only a basket of mud and sand. A third time he cast in his net, and drew out only stones, shells, and filth.

The day now began to dawn, and the fisherman fell to saying his prayers, as his custom was. To them this time he added: "O Lord, Thou knowest that I only throw my net into the sea four times a day. Three times have I done this to-day without a catch. One more only remains. I pray Thee be kind to me as Thou wast to Moses."

For the fourth time the net was thrown. Again there were no fish, but only a copper vase, which seemed to be full of something, for it was very heavy. It was close shut too, and sealed. "I will sell this vase to a founder," said the fisherman, "and, I have no doubt, shall get more money for it than if the net had drawn out a hundred fishes."

First of all he wished to find out what was inside the vase, so, taking his knife, he cut round the edge of the seal, and soon the lid came off. The vase was full of smoke, but, as the fisherman stood gazing at it, the smoke curled out and formed a cloud all round about. Then it came together again, and lo! it took the shape of a genie twice as large as any of the giants.

The fisherman, as you may suppose, tried to run away, but was so afraid that he could not lift a foot.

"Solomon, Solomon," cried the genie. "Pardon, I pray, and I will never more go against thy will."

On hearing this the fisherman grew bold. "What dost thou say, proud spirit?" said he. "Solomon has been dead more than eighteen hundred years. Tell me why thou wast shut up in this vase."

"Speak to me gently," said the genie, "before I kill thee."

"Why wilt thou kill me?" asked the fisherman. "Have I not set thee free? Wilt thou return evil for good?"

"Indeed, I *must* kill thee," said the genie, "but since thou art a good fisherman, I will grant thee one boon."

"What is that?" asked the fisherman.

"You may choose the manner of your death," replied the genie. Then he added, "Listen to my story. King Solomon shut me up in this vase to punish me. He gave the vase to an evil genie, who threw it into the sea. I then made a vow, and said that the person who drew me out in the first hundred years should become a very rich man. Alas! the time went by, and no one drew me out.

"Two other ages also passed by, and still I was not set free. Then, at last, I said I would kill the person who should draw me out, but would grant him the favour to choose how he should die."

"Alack, woe is me!" said the fisherman. "Take back thy vow, and God will forgive you."

"No," said the genie. "Thou must surely die."

The fisherman now felt all in a faint, and was about to fall to the ground. Then he took courage and said to the genie, "I submit to the will of God, but first I must ask you something."

"Be quick then," said the genie. "What is it?"

"I wish to know," said the fisherman, "if you were really in that vase. I cannot believe it. Do you swear it by the great name of God?"

"I swear," said the genie.

"Why," replied the fisherman, with a laugh, "that vase is not big enough to hold one of your feet, let alone all your body, and I shall not think you speak the truth unless you show me."

"Then I will," said the genie, who instantly turned into smoke, and bit by bit curled into the vase.

A voice came out of the smoke. "Do I speak the truth?" asked the genie.

"Wait a bit," said the fisherman, as he quickly put the cover on the vase. "It is now your turn to ask for pardon. But no, I will throw you back into the sea, and on this spot I will build a house and live in it. I will warn all fishermen not to cast their nets hereabouts, and never more shall you be free."

The genie tried hard to move the fisherman to pity, and at last he said, "If you will promise in the great name of God not to harm me I will open the vase."

The genie was ready to promise anything, and did so at once. Then the fisherman took off the cover, and out came the genie.

"Take up your net and follow me," he said, "and I will show you how to get rich."

The two then went away from the city over the top of a high hill to a pond with hills on all its four sides.

"Throw your net into the pond, and catch fish," said the genie.

The fisherman did so, and when he drew out the net, he found he had caught four beautiful fishes, each of a different colour—one red, one white, one blue, and one yellow.

"Take these fishes to the palace," said the genie, "and give them to the Sultan, who will be so pleased with them that he will give you more money than you have ever had in your life.   You may come every day and fish in this pond, but if you cast your net more than once a day, some evil will fall upon you."

When the genie had said this he struck the ground with his foot, and lo! the earth opened and took him from sight.

The fisherman took up his four fishes, and lost no time in going to the palace.

The Sultan was so pleased with the fishes that he said to his porter, "Pray take these four hundred pieces of gold to the fisherman who brought the fishes, and tell him he may bring me four others of the same sort every day of his life at the same price."

This was glad news for the fisherman when he heard it. Never did his family want for food.

THE STORY OF ALI BABA AND THE
FORTY THIEVES

ALI Baba and Cassim were brothers who lived in a
town in Persia. Cassim was rich and famous,
while Ali Baba was so poor that he had to earn
a living by cutting wood and selling it in the
town.

One day when Ali Baba was in the forest he
saw a number of horsemen coming towards him,
and fearing that they might be robbers he quickly
climbed a tree and hid himself.

There were forty in all, and when they came
near the tree where Ali Baba was hiding they
dismounted. After they had tied up their horses
and fed them, they all turned and followed their
captain to a rock near by. "Open Sesame," cried
the leader, and a door opened in the rock. The
men entered one by one, and the captain followed;
then the door closed of itself.

Ali Baba waited, and after some time he saw the
robbers filing out again. When they were out of
sight he went up to the rock and called out
"Open Sesame." The door flew open at the words,
and Ali Baba stepping inside was surprised to find
himself in a well-lighted cavern, filled with all
sorts of valuable goods piled one upon another.
There were bales of silk, rolls of rich carpeting,

heaps of gold and silver ingots, and bags of money.

Ali Baba loaded his asses with some of the gold, and, having covered the bags with his sticks, hurried home to tell his wife of his good fortune. She was overjoyed at the sight of all the money, and wanted to count it; but Ali Baba advised her not to take the trouble, as there was so much. "Then I will borrow a small measure from your brother Cassim and measure it, and while I am away you can be digging a hole for it," she said.

Now, Cassim's wife, knowing how poor her sister-in-law was, felt greatly surprised that she wanted a measure. So, in order to find out what it was for, she slyly put some suet at the bottom of the measure. Ali Baba's wife going home filled it again and again with the gold, and then, being anxious to return the measure as quickly as possible, hurried off with it without noticing that a piece of gold was sticking to the bottom.

Of course, Ali Baba's secret was out, and early next morning, Cassim, going to his brother, threatened to take him before the sheriff if he did not confess the whole truth about the coin. Ali Baba even had to repeat the very words to be used in order to open the door in the rock.

However, although Cassim managed to enter the cave, he was so busy picking up as much treasure as he could and thinking how wealthy he would now be that he quite forgot the magic words. He tried over and over again to remember them; but it was of no use, he only became more confused.

Now, at noon the robbers came, and when Cassim saw the door open he tried to rush out past them, but they quickly put him to death with their swords.

Next day, when Ali Baba came to the cave to look for his brother, he was horrified to find his body cut to pieces, which were hung up just inside the door. As soon as it was dark, he carried the body to his sister-in-law's house, and unloading his ass in the courtyard, told Morgiana, a very sharp and intelligent slave, what was in the bundles.

Morgiana very cleverly spread abroad the news that her master was ill, and later that he was dead. Then she led Mustapha, an old shoemaker, blind-folded to the house, and bribed him well to sew the parts of Cassim's body together. After that Cassim was buried as if he had died a natural death.

Three or four days after the funeral, Ali Baba removed to the widow's house, taking all his own goods during the day; but the money he had removed from the cave he carried at night.

Meanwhile the robbers, when they went to the cave, were amazed to find Cassim's body taken away. They were not only amazed, they were terrified at the thought of having been discovered and of losing their riches.

"We must find the man who knows our secret, and kill him," said the captain decidedly. "The only way in which we can discover him is by keeping a spy in the town, and, to make certain that he will do his work properly, I promise that he shall be put to death if he fails."

Without the least sign of fear, one of the robbers jumped to his feet and offered himself for the task. Every one praised him for his courage, and when he had been well disguised, he was allowed to set out.

In due course he came to the stall of Mustapha, and by means of a number of clever questions found out from the shoemaker that he had lately sewn together the pieces of a dead body.

The robber opened his eyes when he heard this, and asked to be shown the house where such a strange task had been given a shoemaker. Mustapha, on the promise of several pieces of gold, allowed himself to be blindfolded, and with some difficulty managed to lead the way to Cassim's house.

In order that he should not miss the house when he returned with his companions, the robber put a white chalk mark on the door, and having thanked Mustapha, made his way back to the camp. When the captain heard of this success he decided that the robbers should enter the city and slay the man who had learned their secret.

Meanwhile, Morgiana's sharp eyes had seen the mark on her master's door; she could not understand why it was there, but, going out, she made chalk marks exactly the same on several of the neighbours' doors.

So, when the robbers came they could not tell which was the house they were seeking. The captain was very angry, and, thinking the spy had played him a trick, exclaimed, "Let the false guide be put to death! " on which the robber was quickly slain.

In spite of this, however, another came forward and offered to play the spy. He thought that if he marked the door with red chalk in a place not easily to be seen, all would be well. But Morgiana's quick eyes again discovered the mark, and when the robbers came they found so many doors with red marks that they were no further on than before.

The captain at once ordered the second offender to be put to death, and he himself set out to discover the house, with the help of Mustapha. When he had walked up and down in front of it long enough to fix the appearance of it firmly in his memory, he went back to the camp. " Go into all the villages about," he said, "and buy nineteen mules, with thirty-eight large leather jars, one full of oil, and the others empty."

Two days later all was ready. The mules were loaded with thirty-seven robbers in jars and one jar of oil. The captain led the way to the house. Ali Baba was sitting at the door at the time, and when the captain told him that he was on the way to the market with oil, he bade him welcome to his house. The jars were left in the garden, but the captain managed to whisper to the man in each. "When you hear me throw a few stones from my window, make haste to join me."

Fortunately, Morgiana's lamp went out for lack of oil while she was busy at her work, and there was no oil in the house. There seemed nothing for her to do but to go into the garden and take some oil out of the jars. Thus the robber's plot was found out, for instead of oil Morgiana discovered a man in the first jar she opened. "Is it time?" he whispered. "Not yet," she replied softly.

She had to open several jars before discovering the oil, but, as soon as she got it, she ran into the house, filled a kettle with oil, boiled it, and poured enough into every jar to stifle the robber within.

Ali Baba was filled with amazement when he learned next morning that he had been entertaining the captain of the robbers. His gratitude to Morgiana knew no bounds, and he gave her her liberty with the promise of another reward later.

Meanwhile the captain, who had escaped over the wall and returned to his cave, wished to have his revenge on Ali Baba. Accordingly, he started a silk mercer's business, and was overjoyed to discover that Ali Baba's son lived opposite his shop. He gave him presents, invited him to dinner, and did everything he could think of to make friends with him.

Then Ali Baba asked his son's new friend to dine with him. This was the captain's chance. He was known at this time by the name of Cogia Houssain, and at the time appointed Ali Baba's son took him to his father's house. The faithful Morgiana was still there.

Now it happened that as Cogia Houssain said he had made a vow never to touch salt, Ali Baba gave orders to Morgiana to put no salt in the food. Of course, Morgiana could not rest till she had seen this strange visitor who did not like salt, so she helped Abdallah to carry up the dishes.

The first glance at Cogia Houssain told her that he was the captain of the robbers. "I must save my master, or this false merchant will slay him," she said to herself. Going to her room, she put on the dress of a dancer, and fastened round her waist a handsome girdle from which hung a dagger. Thus, having hid her face under a mask, she said to Abdallah, "Bring your tabor, and we will amuse our master and his guest with music and dancing."

Morgiana danced gracefully round and round the room to Abdallah's music, and then suddenly seizing the dagger in her right hand, pretended to stab herself; but as she swept past Cogia Houssain she buried it deep in his breast.

Ali Baba and his son were filled with horror; but when Morgiana opened the pretended Cogia

A.N.

D

Houssain's cloak and showed them a dagger, and told them who he really was, Ali Baba embraced her, and gave her to his son in marriage.

In due course Ali Baba taught his son the secret of the cave, which he in turn handed down to his son, and with the riches they found they were all able to live in comfort and even splendour.

COGIA HASSAN ALHABBAL

ONE day when the Caliph Haroun al Raschid was walking with his grand vizier, both dressed as merchants, through the streets of Bagdad, he saw a very large new house. This, he was told, had been built by one Cogia Hassan, a rope-maker, who had begun life as a very poor man, but who was now one of the richest in the city.

The Caliph, wishing to learn more about him, bade his vizier bring Cogia Hassan to the palace the next day so that he might hear the story of his wonderful rise in life.

Before beginning my story, Cogia said, when brought before the Caliph, I must tell you that in this city there dwell two friends, the one named Saadi and the other Saad, who have always agreed very well except on one subject.

Saadi believes no man can be happy unless he is rich, while Saad says happiness comes not from being rich, but by being good and making the best use of what one has.

One day as they were passing the place in which I carried on my humble trade, they stopped. "Now," said Saad, speaking to his friend, "you have a chance of trying whether riches will make a man happy. Here is a poor rope-maker, who works very hard; yet, by the look of him, he does not seem to be other than a very poor man."

"I am quite willing to take the chance," Saadi answered, "and will do so at once; I always carry with me a sum of money in case I should meet such a person," and then he asked me my name.

"Sir," I answered, "my name is Hassan, and being a rope-maker I am often called Hassan Alhabbal."

"Hassan," said Saadi, "why have you not saved enough money to buy a larger stock of hemp and so have done more trade?"

"Sir," I replied, "I cannot grow rich in that way. I have a wife and five children, and though I work all day long, can earn only enough to keep them in the poorest manner. Still we are content with the little God sends us; and that we have no need to beg makes us happy."

"Hassan," said Saadi, when I had made an end of speaking, "if I give you a purse of two hundred pieces of gold, will you make good use of it, so that you may become as rich as the chief man in your trade?"

Now at first I thought he did but mock me, but, on looking into his face, I saw it was not so. I told him that with a far less sum I would in time become richer than all the rope-makers in Bagdad put together.

Taking a purse from his bosom, "Here is the money then," said he; "I pray God that you may use it well."

With these words he passed on his way, and I, thinking to take good care of the gold, hid it in the folds of my turban. By good luck I kept out ten pieces, with which to buy a large stock of hemp, and some meat for my family who had had none for some days.

Having bought the meat, I was making my way home, carrying it in my hand, when a starving kite flew down and tried to snatch it from me. At last, finding it could not get the meat, it seized my turban and flew off with it.

With some of the money left, I bought myself a new turban, and settled down to my work as I had always been used to do. The rest of the money helped to keep my family in greater comfort than usual, but, when it was all spent, we lived as miserably as before.

However, I did not grumble. God had given us the riches; if it was His will to take them again, I felt we ought not to rebel; but my wife did not see the matter in this way. She made a great trouble of our loss and told the neighbours about it, but they, knowing how poor we had always been, only laughed at her.

About six months afterwards the two friends, Saadi and Saad came to me again, and Saad asked how I was now getting on.

"Gentlemen," I answered sadly, "I am sorry to tell you I have not done as well as you have a right to expect." I then told them about the kite, adding, "You must believe me, for the thing is so

well known in the town that any one will answer
for the truth of the story."

Saad took my part, and in the end Saadi gave me
another purse of two hundred pieces of gold,
bidding me put them in a safer place, and make
good use of them.

As soon as I had thanked him, he walked off
with his friend, and I, putting down my work,
hurried home to hide the gold. My wife and
children were out, so I tied the gold in a linen
cloth, and hid it in a pot of bran. I had, however,
taken from it ten pieces of gold with which, when
my wife came home, I went to buy hemp, of
which I stood in need.

Now, while I was out, my wife, being in want
of sand, and having no money with which to pay
for it, gave the pot of bran to the seller in exchange for the sand.

"Unhappy woman!" I cried, on hearing what
she had done, "you have given the man a hundred
and ninety pieces of gold which I had this after-
noon from my friend Saadi."

My wife was like one mad when she learned the
truth. She cried, and beat her breast, and tore
her hair, blaming herself for her foolishness. In
the hope of calming her, I said, "Do not make so
much noise; the neighbours will hear you, and
laugh at us again. Let us be thankful that we have
the ten pieces of gold with which to provide for
our needs."

So I comforted her, and in time we ceased to

remember our loss; but one day, as I sat working at my trade, I saw Saadi and Saad coming towards me. Feeling ashamed that they should find me no better off than before, I hung my head over my work, pretending to be very busy. But they, instead of passing on, stopped; so, to get over my unpleasant duty as quickly as possible, I told them about the loss of the second sum of money. "Still," I added, "though it is not God's will that I shall grow rich through Saadi's kindness, I am none the less thankful for it."

"Hassan," replied Saadi, "I will try to believe that what you tell me is true, and that you did not spend the money in riotous living; but, while not at all sorry at having given you the four hundred gold pieces, I cannot give you any more."

Then, turning to his friend, he continued, "I own that my idea was not a good one, Saad. It is now your turn to try yours."

Now Saad had a piece of lead in his hand, and this he gave to me, much to the amusement of his friend, who cried, "What can Hassan do with that? It is worth only a farthing!"

But Saad, turning to me, said, "Take it, Hassan, and may it bring you good luck!"

That same night I gave the lead to a fisherman, who, having lost a piece from his net, could not go a-fishing until he had another piece. In return, he brought me a large fish, the first he had taken in his net.

My wife set about cleaning the fish, and, in,

doing so, found what looked like a piece of glass
which she gave to the children for a plaything. It
glittered and sparkled so much that they were
wild with delight, and began to quarrel among
themselves who should play with it most.

They made so much noise that I had to take it
from them. Finding that it gave a very bright
light, I put out the lamp, when the room was lit
up by the light from the glass alone.

"So the bit of lead did bring us luck," I said to
my wife; "this piece of glass will save the money
we spend in oil."

Now, a jeweller and his wife lived next door to
us, and next morning the jeweller's wife asked
why the children had been so noisy at night.
Hearing that it was all about a piece of glass, she
asked my wife to show it her, and, being a good
judge of precious stones, no sooner did she see the
glass than she offered to buy it. But my children
made so much ado about parting with it that she
went away, saying she would speak about it again.

My wife, meanwhile, told me of her wish to buy
the glass, and I, understanding that it must be of
value, agreed to sell it for a hundred thousand
pieces of gold. This, the jeweller paid me, for the
glass was really a diamond of a very rare kind.

Having thanked God for my good fortune, I set
out the next day and visited all the men of my
own trade in the town, giving them orders for as
much work as they could do. Then I hired ware-
houses, and, finding my trade increase, built a

number of workshops, and a large house for myself, on the top of a hill. This is the building you saw yesterday.

My two friends, Saadi and Saad, thinking to find me in my old home, went there, and were sent by the neighbours to my new one. On seeing its size and beauty, they at first thought it could not be mine, but, on my porter assuring them it was indeed so, they entered.

I showed them my fine grounds, and asked them to honour me by spending the night under my roof, to which they agreed. The next morning, as we sat talking in the summer-house, two of my boys came in with a bird's nest built in a turban.

We all looked at it, found it to be the very turban stolen from me by the kite, and, on moving the nest from the turban, there was the purse with the gold pieces I had lost.

Now Saadi, who had never really believed my story, and had been thinking I had grown rich upon his money, seeing the hundred and ninety pieces of gold taken from the turban, was not a little astonished.

"Hassan," said he, "while I doubt not that Saad's piece of lead brought you luck, I am sure that only money makes money."

That evening, it chanced, by some means, that we needed oats, but could get only bran from a small shop near, and my slave, on turning the bran into the mangers, came upon something heavy tied in a linen cloth. This he brought to me, saying it might be the cloth of which he had often heard me speak.

Overjoyed at thus finding the second lot of money, I turned to my guests and said, "Gentlemen, it has pleased God to show you the truth of my words. This is the gold which I tied in the cloth and hid in the pot of bran. You will not wish to have it again, but, with your consent, I will give it to the poor."

"Cogia Hassan," said Caliph Haroun al Raschid, when he had finished his story, "I have not for a long time heard anything that has given me so much pleasure. The diamond you found was bought for my treasury, and, lest Saadi has any doubts in his mind about it, I would have you bring him to my treasurer, who will readily show it him. He may then quite believe that money is not the only means of making a poor man rich."

PRINCE AHMED AND THE FAIRY
PERIE BANOU

THERE was once a sultan who had three sons, Houssain, Ali, and Ahmed. He had also a niece whom he had reared among his own children. Her name was Nouronnihar, and each of the three princes, her cousins, loved her and hoped one day to marry her.

Now the sultan did not wish to favour any of his sons, though he hoped that one of them would become the husband of the princess. He said they should all three travel for a time, and the one who brought back to him the most curious and wonderful thing should marry Nouronnihar.

On a certain day, they set out dressed as merchants, each with an officer clothed as a slave, and carrying a goodly sum of money which their father had given them to pay their expenses, and to spend on buying any rare article they wished to bring home.

On the first day they travelled together till night fell, when they put up at an inn. Before setting out again, they agreed to meet at the same inn at the end of the year, so that they might return together to the palace.

Houssain, after three months of travel over desert, and mountain, and fertile country, at length reached Bisnagar, the chief town of the kingdom of that name which lies on the coast of India. Here he took a room in a khan, in the quarter of the city set apart for foreign merchants.

Everything in Bisnagar showed that the people were very rich. The shops were filled with rare goods, and all the merchants of one trade had their shops in one street.

The buildings were so splendid, and all the goods so costly that Houssain could scarcely believe his own eyes. He walked through the city day after day in the hope of finding something, the like of which had never before been seen, and, one day, while resting in a shop, he heard a man crying a carpet for sale.

Now, as the carpet was small and the price asked very large, Houssain said to the seller, "There must be something strange about the carpet that you ask thirty purses for it! "

"Thirty! " said the man, "nay, I will not sell it for that now. Forty purses must be paid for this magic carpet; why, it will carry anyone who sits on it to any place where he wishes to be."

"If the carpet is what you say," said Houssain, "I will not only give you forty purses for it, but a present for yourself beside."

"Sir," cried the man, "to prove the truth of my words, I will come with you to the inner room of this shop, and sit upon the carpet with you, when, if you so desire, we shall be carried at once to the khan where you lodge.

The merchant having given them leave, Houssain and the seller spread the carpet on the floor of his back shop, when they were at once carried across the city to the khan in which the prince had taken a room.

"Surely," thought Houssain, "the princess will be mine; no one can find a more wonderful thing than this."

He paid the forty purses asked for the carpet, and gave the seller twenty more for himself.

There were still some months to pass before the day came on which he had agreed to meet his brothers, so he resolved to remain in Bisnagar and learn all he could of the manners and customs of the country.

After seeing all the wonders of Bisnagar, Houssain decided to return to the inn. So he bade his officer sit beside him on the magic carpet, and they were at once carried there.

On the day Houssain had set out for the Indian coast, his second brother, Ali, had made his way towards Persia. On the third day he found a caravan, and went with the merchants till they reached Schiraz, which was then the capital of the Kingdom.

Dressed as a jeweller, he took lodgings in a khan among other jewellers. One morning, while walking through that quarter of the city in which jewels and precious stones were sold, he chanced to hear a crier offering for sale an ivory tube about a foot long and an inch thick.

"Thirty purses for the tube!" cried the man, and Ali, going up to a merchant who stood at his shop door, said, "Is the man mad, that he asks thirty purses for so small an article?"

"Indeed no," replied the merchant, "he is one of our best criers. If he asks thirty purses, you may be sure the tube is worth it; but come in and sit down a while; he will pass the door soon, and I will ask him to show you the tube."

"This gentleman," he said to the crier some little time later, "thinks you are out of your senses to ask so much for the tube."

"You are not the only one who thinks me mad," said the crier, turning to Ali; "but the tube is worth more than it appears to be. You see it has glass at both ends, and by looking through one of the glasses you can see anything you desire."

"Tell me through which to look," cried Ali, "and, if your word prove true, I will give you forty purses for the tube."

The crier having shown him, Ali looked through the tube and saw his father sitting on his throne, and surrounded by his council. Then, as he loved Nouronnihar best of any one in the world after his father, he wished to see her. And this he did.

She was sitting at her dressing-table, with her women all about her; and Ali, thinking his present to his father would certainly be the greatest wonder, said to himself, "She will soon be my wife."

He therefore bought the tube, but spent some months in seeing the city and the places round about it before setting out for the inn. On reaching the house he was surprised to find his eldest brother had been there for three months.

"You cannot have gone far," said he to Houssain. When he learned that Houssain had spent three months in reaching the city where he had bought his present and had stayed there for four or five months after buying it, he was puzzled to know how he had got back to the inn.

"Unless you flew here, I cannot understand it," he said.

"I cannot explain," Houssain replied, "until Ahmed comes; then I will tell you."

Both the brothers were just as much puzzled about what each had bought, but, although they said nothing, each felt sure of winning the princess by the strangeness of his gift.

Now Ahmed had taken the road to Samarcande on the morning when the brothers set out on their travels, and, falling in with some travelling jewellers, he dressed himself as they did, and went with them, on reaching the city, to their inn.

The next day, in the part of the town given up to the traders, he heard a man crying an apple for sale. It was not a real apple. It had been made by a very clever doctor, who died before he could use it himself as the crier declared it could be used.

"This apple," said the crier, "has the power to cure all diseases; even were a man almost dead, it would bring him back to life and good health."

"If what you say is true," said Ahmed, "I will pay you forty purses for the apple."

Now it chanced that a man in the crowd had a friend who was very ill, so the crier went to the sick man's house and cured him of his sickness. Ahmed then paid him the forty purses asked for the apple, and took it away in great joy, "For," thought he, "there can be nothing more wonderful than this in all the world."

After spending a little time in seeing the beautiful parts of the kingdom of Samarcande, Ahmed joined the first caravan starting for the Indies, and in good time reached the inn where his brothers awaited him.

The greeting being over, Houssain said to his brothers, "There will be plenty of time later to speak of our travels; let us now show each other the curious things we have bought. This carpet is so wonderful that I believe you will both think it the strangest thing of which you have ever heard. It will carry whoever sits on it to any place, far or near, to which he may wish to go.

"I paid forty purses for it in Bisnagar, and when I was ready to leave the city, the carpet was the carriage which brought my servant and me here. I will allow you to see the carpet at work whenever you please."

"I must own," said Ali, when Houssain had made an end of speaking, "that the carpet is a most surprising thing; but there are others quite as

wonderful. This ivory tube will allow you to see
any one you wish, simply by looking through the
glass at one end of it. Take it, and judge for yourself."

Houssain, to whom Ali had offered the tube,
took it, and wishing to see Nouronnihar, and to
know if she were well and happy, looked through
the glass, when his face became full of trouble.

"Alas, brothers," he cried, "the charming princess whom we all love so much is about to die.
Take the glass, and you will see her in bed, with
all her servants standing round and weeping."
When Ali had looked at Nouronnihar, Ahmed
took the glass and, having taken one glance at the
dying princess, said, "It is true; she is at death's
door; but if we can reach her quickly, we may
save her life. This apple has the power to cure any
disease; the person who smells it, even though
dying, will be restored to health and strength. I
have seen its power, and am sure it will save
Nouronnihar if we can get to her in time."

"Come, then," said Houssain, "the carpet will
just hold the three of us; but first we must direct
our servants to join us at the palace."

Seating themselves on the carpet, they all wished
to be carried to their cousin's room. Their
arrival at the palace caused no little surprise, for
they had not been expected; but Prince Ahmed no
sooner found himself in Nouronnihar's bedroom
than he went to her side and put the apple to her
nose.

In a few minutes she opened her eyes, sat up in bed, and, speaking as though newly wakened from a sound sleep, asked to be dressed.

Her women, however, told her how much she owed to her three cousins, and most of all to Ahmed, but for whom she would surely have died. Nouronnihar thanked them, and they, saying how glad they were to have helped her, went to the sultan, their father, to show him the wonderful things they had brought.

Now the sultan had heard that Nouronnihar, whom he loved as a daughter, had been cured by the apple, but he listened to his sons' stories with great attention.

"It is true," he said, when they had finished speaking, "that Ahmed's apple cured the princess, but it was Ali's tube that told you she was ill, and Houssain's carpet that brought you here in time to save her. Thus each article is as wonderful as the other, and neither the princess nor myself can choose between them. I must find some other way of deciding whose wife she shall be.

"Fetch your bows and arrows, and meet me on the great plain beyond the city. I will give Nouronnihar to him who shoots the farthest. I thank you all for the gifts you have brought, and shall look after them with great care."

Having taken each his bow and arrow, the three princes, followed by many people, went to the plain. Houssain, being the eldest, shot first, Ali second and Ahmed last. Ahmed's arrow seemed to

go farthest; but, as it could not be found, the
sultan said Nouronnihar should be given to Ali,
whose shot had been longer than that of Houssain, and the wedding took place a few days
afterwards.

Houssain at once gave up all right to the crown,
and became a dervish, and Ahmed stole away to
seek the arrow he had lost. Going to the great
plain, he travelled on and on till, reaching some
steep rocks, he found the missing arrow.

"Surely," he said to himself, "there is something very strange in this, for no man living could
shoot an arrow so far. Perhaps what I have thought
my greatest sorrow may be turned into my
greatest joy after all."

Seeing an opening in the rocks he passed
through, when, lo! there appeared before him an
iron door that had no lock. With a slight push it
flew open, and Prince Ahmed, entering, found
himself in the courtyard of a most beautiful
palace. Just as he reached the porch, a beautiful
lady, with many others quite as lovely, came
torwards him, saying, "Come near, Prince Ahmed,
you are welcome."

Now, as Ahmed had never before seen or heard
of the lady, he felt some surprise that she knew
him. Having bowed low before her, he replied,
"Madam, I thank you for your kind welcome;
but will you do me the favour of telling me how
you know me, when I have never even heard of
you?"

"Prince," answered the beautiful lady, "if you will come into the hall, where we shall be more comfortable, I will tell you."

"You are surprised," she said, after they were seated on a splendid sofa, "that I know you; yet I know your brothers also, and the travels you undertook in order to win the Princess Nouronnihar. It was I who caused to be put up for sale the three articles you and they bought. It was I, also, who carried your arrow so far away, as I wished to give you greater happiness than you would have had as the husband of Nouronnihar.

"It is not strange that you know nothing of me, as I am a fairy. My name is Perie Banou, and I am the daughter of a genie. In our world it is the custom for the ladies to propose marriage, and, as I love you, and am willing to marry you, I hope you will be my husband."

Now Prince Ahmed had fallen in love with the fairy on first seeing her; so he was quite as willing to marry her as she had hoped he would be. The wedding was a very simple one, as all weddings are in fairyland. Before the marriage feast was ready, Perie Banou took the prince through all the halls and rooms in her splendid palace; and Prince Ahmed no longer envied his brother Ali.

He thought Perie Banou was more beautiful, more agreeable, and far more wealthy than the princess, his cousin; so for six months he lived at her palace in great happiness. At the end of that time, however, he began to wish to see his father, and said so to his wife; but she, fearing he might not return, begged him not to leave her.

Now Ahmed really loved his wife with all his heart, so he yielded to her wish. Often, however, as they sat talking, he spoke of his father, for whom he had great affection, and who, he feared, was sorely troubled at his long absence.

Indeed, this was so; as the sultan grieved very much for his youngest son. On hearing he had left the palace, he had sent to all the countries near, asking that if his son had been seen anywhere, he should at once be sent back to his home.

In spite of all his care, nothing was heard of Prince Ahmed, so at last, sending for his grand vizier, he said to him, "Vizier, you know that Ahmed was my best loved son. I am so troubled about him that I shall surely die. Help me, therefore, for pity's sake, to find him."

On this, the vizier, who had a great regard for the sultan, sent for a certain witch, by whose aid, perhaps, the prince might be found.

The witch came in a little time, and, having heard what was wanted, said, "Give me until to-morrow. I may then perhaps be able to help you."

But, on the next day, all she could tell the sultan of his lost son was, that he still lived, and with this he had to be content.

At last, the fairy, seeing how truly Ahmed loved her, and the wish he still had to see his father, agreed to let him go, if he would promise not to make too long a stay, nor to tell his father of his marriage.

"Beg him," she said, "to believe that you are happy; that you could wish nothing more than you have, and tell him you came back only to set his mind at rest about you."

Mounted on a fine horse, and with twenty men, all well mounted and clothed, Prince Ahmed at length set out for his father's palace, which was not far away. As he rode slowly into the city, he was followed by crowds of people, even into the presence of his father.

The sultan met him with great joy, but could not keep from asking why he had left the court in so great a hurry.

"Sir," replied Ahmed, "it was not good that I should stay to see the happiness of my brother Ali, so I set out to find the lost arrow. And this I did. The arrow lay upon the ground at the foot of some steep rocks, on the farther side of the great plain, and I thought there was meaning in the flight of the arrow that might lead to my happiness.

"So it proved to be; for, without leaving the spot, I became very happy, and my only reason for returning is that you might cease to worry about me. I beg you to ask no questions, for I may answer none; only give me leave to come often and see you."

The sultan would have liked to learn his son's secret, but he understood this could not be; so he begged Ahmed to come whenever he would, saying that it would be a great joy to see him.

On the fourth day Ahmed returned to the fairy, who gave him leave to visit his father once every month. This he did, going each time in richer clothing and with more gaily dressed officers. The sultan was always full of joy at his coming, but some of the viziers, jealous of Ahmed's wealth, at length tried to set his father against him. "Some day," said they, "the people will make him their ruler in your place."

"You are mistaken," the sultan answered; "my son loves me, and I have faith in him."

But they, far from letting the matter rest, lost no chance of making him believe that Ahmed meant to turn him off the throne. Though not letting them see how their words troubled him, he could not help thinking of them when in the quiet of his own room. At last he made up his mind to send for the witch again.

"You were right," he said to her, "in saying my son Ahmed was alive. For that I thank you. I now want you to do me another favour. I have seen him many times lately, but I cannot discover where he lives. He is here at this moment, but, as I never know when he goes away, I pray you wait in the road, watch well where he goes, and tell me."

Now the witch knew well where the prince had found his arrow, so she went there, and hid among the rocks till he came with his servants. She watched carefully; but all at once they went out of sight, and though she looked again and again about the hollow, she could find no opening of any kind.

Going back to the sultan she told him all she had seen. "But," she added, "I will not now tell you what I think. When I am quite sure about it I will let you know, but you must ask no questions as to how I found it out."

"Do as you think fit," the sultan replied. "I will await your news. Take this diamond; it is a small payment for what you have done; when you have found the secret I will pay you much more."

Knowing that Prince Ahmed always visited his father once a month, the witch made up a cunning plan. Going to the rocks a day or two before the time of starting she waited, and, as soon as she saw him drawing near, laid her head upon the rocks as if in great pain.

"Good woman," said the prince, riding to the spot where she lay; "get up behind one of my servants; I will take you where you will be well cared for."

Upon this the witch tried to rise, and the prince, thinking she was really ill, told two of his men to set her on a horse and bring her into the fairy's palace.

"My princess," he said to his wife, who was surprised to see him return so soon, "I found this woman lying sick upon the road. I pray that she may be given the help which she needs."

The princess, telling two of her women to take the witch into a certain room and attend to her, replied, "Prince, I am glad to see you so kind-hearted, but I fear trouble will come from this. The woman is not so sick as she pretends; but do not be uneasy, I will guard you against all the traps laid for you."

"My princess," said Ahmed, nothing moved by the fears of his wife, "I have never done wrong to anyone in my life, and I do not think anyone would try to wrong me."

With these words, he once more started for his father's court, where he was warmly greeted, as usual, while the sick woman was tended with great care by those into whose charge she had been given. They carried her into a grand room, and put her into a bed with the finest linen sheets and a gold coverlet.

They gave her a drink from a cup of priceless china, and when she asked to be taken to their mistress to thank her, they led her through halls filled with costly furniture to one in which Perie Banou sat upon a throne of massy gold.

"Good woman," said the fairy, on seeing her, "I am glad to have been of use to you, and to know that you are now able to continue your journey; but, before you go, you may like to see my palace —my women will show it to you."

Led by these women, who were themselves fairies, the witch passed through halls whose splendour drew from her many cries of delight, and yet this was but a small part of the fairy's wealth. At last they let her out at the iron door through which she had entered, but, though she tried her best to find it again, after it had been shut, she could not do so.

However, as this was the only thing in which she had failed, she went to tell her news to the sultan.

After telling her story she added, "I fear this fairy, to whom you son is married, may lead him into wishing to rule in your stead, and this is a serious matter, which your majesty would do well to consider."

Now the sultan had been told this so often that he was beginning to believe it; therefore, bidding the witch follow him into his council chamber, he told his favourite ministers all he had learned.

"Sir," said one of them, "I advise you to take the prince prisoner and to keep him shut up for the rest of his life."

"Sir," said the witch, thinking this would be unwise, "if you keep the prince, you must also keep his servants. This you cannot do, because they are all genies. They will fly at once to the palace of the fairy and tell her, when she will find some means to punish you.

"If you take my advice you will ask your son to bring you, by the aid of his fairy wife, so many wonderful things that he will at last grow tired and shut himself up for life in his palace. In this

way you will be saved the crime of killing your
own son, or even of making him a prisoner."

The sultan made up his mind to act on this
advice, and the next time Ahmed came into his
room, he said, "Son, though you have never told
me your secret, I know of your marriage with the
rich and powerful fairy. I am pleased you have
done so well, and hope you will obtain for me
your wife's help whenever I need it. I want you to
ask her to send me a tent small enough to be
carried on a man's hand, yet large enough to
shelter a whole army. It is not easy to get, but I
feel sure she will get it for your sake."

Now, though fairies can do many things im-
possible to men, Prince Ahmed felt that such a
thing as his father asked could not be made even
by them. Besides, he did not like to ask his wife for
any such favours, so he replied, "Sir, it is true I
have married the fairy, though I know not how
you found it out. I hope you will not insist on
my asking this favour of her; yet, if I must ask
it, I will. Should I come not again, you will
understand that I have failed to obtain it."

"Son," replied the sultan, "people often lose
things for want of asking. You do not yet know
what your wife will do to show her love for you.
Ask her for the tent; if she does not give it to you,
she does not love you as she ought."

To this Ahmed made no reply. He was very
vexed and left the palace two days earlier than
usual. On reaching home, his face was still

troubled, so that his wife, who looked always to see him return in a gay mood, asked what had happened to make him sad.

"Tell me," she said, "and whatever the cause, I will try to remove it. Perhaps the sultan, your father, is dead; if so, I will do all I can to comfort you."

"Thanks be to God," said Ahmed, "my father is alive and well, but, in spite of all my care, he has found out about our marriage."

"I know who told him," cried the fairy. "Did I not say that sick woman would bring us trouble? It is she who has told him. But tell me, what does your father wish? Do not fear; you cannot ask too much of me."

"Madam," said the prince, "though for myself I would never ask any other favour than your love, my father wishes you to send him a tent large enough to shelter his whole army, yet small enough to be carried in a man's hand."

"Prince," replied the fairy smiling, "let so small a matter cease to trouble you; I can easily do that, and, believe me, I shall always take pleasure in doing anything whatever, for your sake."

Then, bidding a servant bring the largest tent in the place, she laughed at the look of surprise on her husband's face when the tiny thing was brought.

"Go, set it up," she said, "that the prince may see if his father will think it large enough."

The tent proved to be even larger than his

father wished, and Ahmed asked his wife's pardon
for doubting her power.

"There is one thing to notice," she said in reply,
"the tent becomes larger or smaller, as it is
needed, without anything more being done to it."

When it was taken down and made small again,
she gave it to the prince, who, the very next day,
took it to his father.

The sultan's surprise was great when Ahmed
placed the tent in his hands. Taking it to the great
plain, he put it up, when it became large enough
to cover an army twice the size of his own. However, instead of being pleased, he felt it showed that
the fairy's power was great enough to do anything she wished.

He sent his best thanks by his son, and asked her
to send him a little of the water of the fountain of
lions, which was said to cure all disease, so that
if he were taken ill he might have a remedy at
hand.

Prince Ahmed was much vexed, but, on telling
his wife, she agreed to send it. "For," said she, "I
see he listens to the witch, and whatever she tells
him to ask, I will grant. The fountain of lions is
in the court of the castle, and the entrance is
guarded by four lions. Do not fear; I will give
you a piece of thread, two horses—one of which
you must ride while leading the other laden with
the carcase of a sheep cut into four quarters—and
a bottle in which to carry the water.

"You must set out early to-morrow morning,

and, on passing the iron gate, throw the thread until it reaches the castle gates; the gates will open, and you will see the lions. Throw to each a quarter of the sheep, clap spurs to your horse, and ride to the fountain. Fill the bottle, and return while the lions are still feasting."

Prince Ahmed started the next morning, and did just as his wife had told him. He was coming back again, when chancing to look behind, he saw two of the lions following him. They did not touch him, but, placing themselves one before and the other behind him, went as far as the gates of the palace, and then returned.

As soon as the sultan had the bottle, "Son," he said, "I thank you for the water, but pray tell me how you got safely away from the lions of whom I have heard."

"Sir," replied Ahmed, "all the praise is due to my wife, whose orders I have carried out."

Then the sultan, going into another room, sent for the witch, who advised him to ask Ahmed to bring him a man not more than a foot and a half high, whose beard should be thirty feet long, and who should carry on his shoulders a bar of iron weighing five hundred-weight, and who should be able to speak.

"If you do this," said the sultan to his son the next day, "I will ask no further favours from you or your wife."

Ahmed went home in a rather troubled state of mind, for he thought this last favour would be too

hard, even for her to grant. But the fairy set his
mind at rest.

"My brother Schaibar," she said, "is just such
a man. I will send for him, and you shall see I
speak truly."

A golden chafing-dish with a fire in it having
been placed under the porch of the palace, the
fairy threw some incense upon it, when out of the
thick cloud there came a man, only a foot and a
half high, with a beard thirty feet long, and carrying a huge iron bar on his shoulder. He was so
ugly that Prince Ahmed would have been filled
with fear, but that he knew him to be his wife's
brother.

"Who is that man?" asked Schaibar, coming
towards Perie Banou with a fierce scowl on his
face.

On learning that Ahmed was her husband,
Schaibar asked in what way he could serve him,
and being told of the sultan's wish to see him,
agreed to go with Ahmed to the palace.

"You wished to see me," he said to the king,
"what can I do for you?"

Instead of answering, the sultan turned his head
away; and Schaibar, being angry at such rude-
ness, struck him on the head and killed him,
before Ahmed could do anything to stop him.
Then he put to death those who had set Ahmed's
father against him, even bidding the grand vizier
bring out the witch, that she, too, might be
punished for the evil she had done.

Schaibar next called out the people and made them swear to own Ahmed as their king, and Perie Banou as their queen. This they did very willingly, for they had always loved the young prince. When Ahmed found that neither Ali nor his wife had had anything to do with the plot against him, he gave him a large part of the kingdom, where they spent the rest of their lives. Houssain would not return, though Ahmed offered him the best of the country. All he asked of his brother was leave to live in peace on the spot he had chosen for his dwelling.

THE STORY OF PRINCE CAMARALZAMAN
AND PRINCESS BADOURA

ABOUT twenty days' sail from the coast of Persia there is an island which is called the Isle of the Children of Khaledan.

The island was ruled by King Schahzaman, who had a son named Camaralzaman. Camaralzaman was a good young prince and clever too, for he learnt without trouble all things which a prince ought to know. His father was very proud of him.

When the prince was fifteen years of age the king went to his grand vizier and said to him, "I am very proud of my son Camaralzaman, and I want to do him all the honour I can. I intend to give up my throne and let him take my place."

The vizier did not think this was a very good plan, for a king who was only fifteen years of age would not rule a kingdom so well as an older one. So he said to the king, "Let him marry first, and then we shall see what kind of a man he will make."

This idea pleased the king very much, and he sent for Camaralzaman without delay. When the prince had come to him the king said, "My son,

E

I wish you to marry. What do you think of it? "

Now Prince Camaralzaman had taken a dislike to ladies, and had made up his mind never to have a wife. "Sire," said he to his father, "don't you think I had better wait for a year or two before I choose a wife? I am much too young to marry."

"Very well," said the king. "I will give you time to think of it."

A full year went by, and then the king sent for Camaralzaman again. "Now, my son," said the king, "you are quite old enough to have a wife. What have you to say? "

"I have not yet thought of such a thing, indeed I haven't, Father," replied Camaralzaman.

The king was sore vexed, but, not wishing to punish his son, he sent for his vizier. "What shall I do? " he asked. "My son tells me he will not choose a wife."

The vizier said that he thought another year should be given to the prince and if at the end of that time he should still refuse, he should be made to marry.

The king agreed with his vizier that this would be a wise plan.

That year went by, but still Camaralzaman would not choose a wife. The king then asked Camaralzaman's mother to talk to him about it; and although that lady did so, Camaralzaman was still of the same mind. "I won't marry," said he. And he meant what he said.

The king once more called his vizier. "My son

still refuses to marry," said the king, "and I am going to punish him."

The vizier bowed seven times, which was a sign that he thought the prince ought to be punished. Camaralzaman was called, and the king said to him, "Camaralzaman, my son, you take no notice of my wishes. You must leave the palace, and go to live all by yourself in the tall tower. You shall have a bed, some books, and one slave to attend to you. That is all. Go."

Prince Camaralzaman was not in the least vexed at this. On the other hand, he was rather pleased to be alone. When night came he lay down on his bed quite content, and fell fast asleep. He left his lamp burning.

Now, in the tower was a well, and in the well there dwelt a fairy whose name was Maimounè. The same night that Camaralzaman lay on his bed for the first time Maimounè came up the well ready to go her nightly rounds. She saw the light burning, and went up to the couch.

"What a handsome youth," said she, "and what a pity he will not marry." Then she stooped down and kissed his cheek. After that she flew into the air, where she met a genie.

"O genie," said the fairy, "where have you come from to-night?"

"I have come from China," said the genie, "And I have seen there a fine sight. The king is Gaiour, and he has a most lovely daughter, the most beautiful princess in the world.

"Gaiour loves the princess dearly, and has built for her seven palaces. The first is of rock crystal, the second of bronze, the third of the finest steel, the fourth of another kind of bronze, the fifth of touchstone, the sixth of silver, and the seventh of fine gold.

"There are gardens and lawns round the palaces, the whole forming a very grand place.

"The kings from all the country round want the hand of the princess in marriage, but Gaiour cannot make up his mind upon whom to bestow it, and the princess does not want to marry at all.

"Gaiour has told his daughter that she must marry some one, but she won't. I heard her say to the king, ' Speak to me no more, sire, of such a thing as marriage. If you do, I will plunge a dagger into my heart and be free.

"That, as you may suppose, made the king very angry, and he shut her up in a single room, and gave her only ten slaves to wait on her. Nay, more. The king thinks she is mad, and has said he will give a large reward, as well as the hand of the princess, to any one who can cure her.

"Come with me, and I will show her to you."

At this the fairy laughed. "I thought you were going to tell me something very nice," she said. "I have just seen a far more handsome prince than you have seen a lovely princess."

"That cannot be true," said the genie.

Then it was agreed that the genie should go to China and fetch the princess, who, when she was brought, should be taken to Camaralzaman's tower and laid down by his side. Very soon the genie came back with the princess.

As the two lay on the couch it was plain that they were both very beautiful. The fairy and the genie looked at them, but could not make up their minds which was the more lovely.

Just at that moment Prince Camaralzaman awoke, and seeing the princess by his side, looked into her face. "What beauty! what charms! Oh, my heart, my soul!" said he. "This is without doubt the lady whom my father wishes me to marry. What a pity I did not see her sooner!"

He was then about to kiss her on the forehead, but thinking he might wake her—a thing he did not wish to do—he took her ring from her finger and changed it for his own. Then he fell as fast asleep as he was before.

Not long afterwards the princess awoke and looked round the room. She did not know where she was. Then she reached out her hand and felt the prince.

She started with surprise, and looking at him, saw that he was the most handsome young man she had ever seen in her life. "What!" said she to herself, "is this the person my father wishes me to marry? I will wake him and talk to him. No. I will take his ring and wear it on my own finger."

But before she could do this she fell fast asleep again.

The genie and the fairy had watched all this

without being seen by the prince or princess. When the two were once more fast asleep, the genie carried the princess home to her own room, and laid her down on her own couch.

When Prince Camaralzaman awoke next morning he looked for the princess. Lo! she was not there. He called his slave and asked him what had become of her. Of course, the slave did not know there had been a princess in the room at all, so he told him he must have had a dream. On this Prince Camaralzaman beat the slave soundly, who, as soon as he could, made his escape, and went and told the king what the prince had whipped him for.

The vizier was there, but neither he nor the king could make out what the slave was talking about. Then the king went to the tower. "What is this I hear, my son?" asked the king.

Camaralzaman told his father about the beautiful princess, and said he would marry her at once. The king said he did not know of any princess, and thought his dear son was mad. For many days Prince Camaralzaman was sad, and no one could comfort him.

Now while all these things were taking place in the court of King Schahzaman, very much the same was happening in China. The princess, whose name was Badoura, awoke and called in a loud voice for her maidens. They rushed to her, and she asked them where the prince was.

"Prince?" they asked. "What prince?"

"The prince who lay on my couch last night,"
said Badoura. "If you do not tell me at once, I
will beat you every one."

Not one of the maidens could tell the princess
what she wanted to know. Then the princess took
the chief maiden, who was her nurse, by the hair
and gave her many slaps and blows. As soon as
she could get away she ran to the queen and told
her the strange story.

The queen went to see her daughter, and so did
the king. They knew nothing about a prince, and
both thought their dear daughter was mad. She
showed them the ring which Camaralzaman had
placed on her finger, and that was a strange thing
to them.

For many days the princess was sad, and no one
could comfort her.

The King of China could not endure to see his
daughter suffer so. He gave out that if any one
could cure her complaint he should wed her for
his pains. This was the second time.

Many princes tried to cure her, but they could
not. Indeed, so many tried one after the other that
the king said he who should try and fail should
have his head struck off. This kept some from
trying, but in the end there were one hundred and
fifty heads stuck on the walls of the city.

Still the princess was sad.

Now the nurse of the princess had a son whose
name was Marzavan. He was a clever young man,
and had been in many cities of the world. He

came home from his travels, and heard the strange story of the princess.

Marzavan got leave to see the princess, and he told her that he hoped he would find a cure if she would wait a few days. He meant to travel till he should find some clever doctor.

Next day, losing no time, he set out. As he went from city to city he could hear nothing but the story of the Princess Badoura and the prince's ring, and the reward the man should get who should cure her of her madness.

Marzavan came at last to a city where no one talked of Badoura, but of Prince Camaralzaman and the ring of a princess. "This is strange," thought he to himself. "I must see this Camaralzaman; perhaps he will be the very prince whom Badoura wants to marry."

Off he set once more, but the ship he was in was wrecked just as she was going into the port of the city where Prince Camaralzaman lived. Marzavan was a good swimmer, and he soon reached the shore. He found his way to the court of King Schahzaman, where he heard the full story of the prince and the ring from no less a person than the vizier himself.

"May I see the prince?" asked Marzavan. "You may, of course," said the vizier, who led the way to Prince Camaralzaman's chamber.

The moment Marzavan saw the prince he was struck by his face. It was handsome, and just like the Princess Badoura's. He started, and Prince

Camaralzaman called him to his side. Then Marzavan knew his journey would not be in vain. He felt sure he had found the proper person.

Marzavan spoke to him in a low voice and said, "Prince, the time is come when you must put an end to your sadness. The lady for whom you suffer is well known to me; she is the Princess Badoura, daughter of the King of China, whose name is Gaiour. The princess is even now mourning for you."

Then he told the prince all about the reward King Gaiour had said he would give to the one who could cure his daughter, and added, "You, prince, are the only person who can cure her. Make haste to get well, and you shall try your luck."

Hope came at once to Prince Camaralzaman. No sooner had he heard the words of Marzavan than he seemed to get better. He rose from his couch, and let himself be dressed. In a few days he was quite well.

Then a new trouble came to him, for he felt sure his father, the king, would not be willing for him to travel so far as China. "What shall I do?" asked he of Marzavan.

"Leave that to me," said Marzavan. "I am quite sure I can manage a small matter like that." And he did, for in a day or two he made a party for a hunt, and when the prince and he were alone he said to the prince, "Now, prince, is your chance. Let us flee."

Away they went and soon left the other hunts-men out of sight. When they came at last to the sea they took ship, and in a good many days reached the city where Princess Badoura lived.

Prince Camaralzaman changed his dress, and made out that he was a wise man from a far-off land who had come to cure the princess of her madness. He was told by the people that he had better not try, for he would be sure to lose his head like the others who had tried. But he paid no heed to their words.

Soon the Vizier led Camaralzaman into the king's chamber. The king said to him, "Young man, I hardly dare think you can cure my daughter, but you may try. Take care, or your head will be struck off."

"Sire," said the prince, "the land where I come from has many wise men. I know the arts of all cures, and I am ready to restore your daughter to health and happiness. If not, I am just as ready for death."

The king then gave orders for Camaralzaman to be taken to the princess. When he got near her chamber he was so overjoyed to think he should soon see his darling again that he ran on in front of his guide.

"Where are you going, good sir?" asked he, "You must be very ready to die to run so fast into the arms of death."

"Friend," said Camaralzaman, "I am sure to cure the princess."

Oh, how his heart beat! He could hear the princess in her chamber moaning and he longed to be with her. But he said to his guide, "I am so sure of curing the princess that I will do it in which way you think best. I will speak to her from here, or I will go in and see her."

"I do not care in the least how you do it," said the guide. "I only know that if you do it at all you will be the wisest man in the world."

Then the prince drew from his belt some paper, on which he wrote these words: "Prince Camaralzaman to the Princess of China—Dear Princess, the heart-broken Prince Camaralzaman sends you word that he gave you his heart during your sweet sleep. He placed your ring on his finger in token of his love. He is outside your room. If you love him, come to him. If you do not, he will die."

Prince Camaralzaman gave the paper to his guide and told him to take it to the princess. The guide looked at the note in wonder, but took it in.

In a moment the note was broken open and read. Then the princess dashed past her maidens into the ante-chamber. She knew the prince at once, and fell into his embrace. Not a word was spoken, but they knew each loved the other.

The princess was a new creature. She looked happy and smiled. Her nurse was glad, and the guide ran off to tell the king what the stranger had done. "He has cured her," said he, "without even seeing her."

How glad the king was! "Whoever you may be," said he to Camaralzaman, "I will keep my promise. You may wed the princess without delay."

Then Camaralzaman told the king who he was, and that his father was the King of the Isle of the Children of Khaledan. He also told the king the story as he had heard it from his daughter, and showed him the princess's ring in proof.

That very day Prince Camaralzaman and the Princess Badoura were wed, and the whole land of China was happy, but in the night the prince dreamed that his father was sick and sad at the loss of his son. He awoke with a deep sigh, which waked the princess.

"Why weepest thou, my love?" asked she.

"Alas!" cried the prince, "I know that my father mourns my loss. We must both go to him."

The King of China gave his leave for his daughter and his son-in-law to journey to King Schahzaman, but said they must both come back in a year.

As soon as they could get ready they set out, and one evening camped near a forest. The princess was tired, and lay down to sleep. Her maidens had taken off her girdle so that she might rest at ease. There it lay near her couch.

Camaralzaman looked at it and admired the many jewels which were on it. Then he saw that a little purse was stitched to the inside, and that it had something hard in it. He opened it, and lo, there was a cornelian in it—a precious stone which the queen, the princess's mother, had given to her as a charm.

In order to look at the cornelian more closely, Prince Caramalzaman took it to the tent door, when all at once a bird darted down from the air and carried it off in his beak.

"Wretched bird!" said Camaralzaman and started after it in the hope of getting back the stone. The bird flew a little way and then stopped. Camaralzaman was about to seize it when it flew off again. This went on for a long time, and Camaralzaman had not yet caught the bird. Night came on, and the bird perched on a high tree.

The prince dared not go back to his princess without the stone, so he laid himself down at the foot of the tree and slept.

Next day he again gave chase to the bird, and for the next ten days. On the eleventh he came to a large city, over the walls of which the bird flew and was lost to sight.

Poor Camaralzaman! what could he do? He thought of his wife, yet knew not how to get back to her. He had quite lost his way. He walked into the city and along the streets. On and on he went till he came to a garden, the gate of which was open.

The gardener was at work, and when he saw Camaralzaman he asked him to shelter in his cottage, telling him that the people of the city were very unkind to strangers.

Camaralzaman was glad to rest, and after a little time he told the gardener why he had come there. The gardener said it was a year's journey to the Isle of the Children of Khaledan, and that a ship went once a year. "If you had been here a few days sooner," said he, "you could have gone by ship. Now you must wait a twelvemonth. You may stay with me in my cottage."

Let us now turn to the Princess Badoura. For a long time she waited in her camp at the edge of the forest, but as the prince did not return she had to go on without him.

Now, in that land it was not safe for a party to be in charge of a lady, so the princess put on a suit of Prince Camaralzaman's clothes, and bade one of her maidens dress as a princess and pretend to be her.

On they went, and in six months came to the city of the Isle of Ebony. There the people thought that the princess was a prince, and led her to the king, whose name was Armanos. Princess Badoura told the king that she was Prince Camaralzaman, and that she was going to her father's court.

King Armanos was pleased to have so handsome a prince, as he thought, at his palace, and when the princess had stayed there three days he gave her in marriage to his own daughter.

What a fix Princess Badoura was in to be

sure! She had said that she was Prince Camaralzaman, and if she now said she was a princess,
King Armanos might put her to death. So she
let herself be married to King Armanos' daughter.

When the two were in their chamber at night
Princess Badoura told her wife who she was, and
begged her to keep her secret. She said she would,
and that she hoped the Princess Badoura might
soon find her husband. Thus they lived for some
time.

Prince Camaralzaman worked with the gardener in the garden. One day, when the yearly
ship was about to sail for the Isle of Ebony,
the gardener went to secure a passage for the
prince. While he was away a strange thing took
place.

Two birds came into the garden where Prince
Camaralzaman was at work. They pecked at each
other with all their might, till at last one of them
dropped dead. The other flew away, but in a few
minutes, two birds who had watched the fight
from a high tree fetched him back and pecked
him so much that he died on the spot where he had
killed the other bird.

Prince Camaralzaman then went to this second
dead bird, and what should he find in his body but
the cornelian for which he had so long sought.

His joy was great, as you may suppose. He took
it up and tied it to his arm so that he might never
lose it again. Then he set to work with a will.
While he was cutting at the root of a tree which

no longer bore fruit, his axe struck something hard and made a loud noise.

Looking closely, he saw that he had opened a cave in the ground, and that in the cave were fifty large bronze jars. Each was filled with gold dust of great value.

The gardener now came back and said that Camaralzaman might sail for home in a few days, whereupon Camaralzaman told the gardener what he had found in the bird and in the cave. The gardener would not take any share in the gold dust, but said that as Camaralzaman had found it he ought to have it all.

For safety, some olives were put into the jars to cover up the gold, and into one of them Camaralzaman put the cornelian also, for safety.

Just then some sailors came to the prince and told him all was ready for the voyage, and that he must go on board that night.

It came to pass that night, however, that the gardener was taken ill and died. Prince Camaralzaman was so struck with grief at the sudden loss of his friend that he missed the ship, and it set sail without him. Another year must now pass by before he could embark.

The seamen carried away the jars of gold and the cornelian too, so that Prince Camaralzaman was in a worse plight than before.

The ship sailed to the Isle of Ebony, where the Princess Badoura saw it going into the harbour. She sent to ask whence it had come and what it had brought. She learnt that it was stored with all sorts of fine dresses and stuffs, and some jars of olives. She was also told that the merchant who owned the olives was left behind and had not sailed.

The princess bought the olives from the captain of the ship and they had them taken to the palace. When they were opened, lo! there was found in them the gold and the cornelian.

With surprise and joy she fainted away; but the princess of the Isle of Ebony and her maidens ran to her help and soon brought her round. She took the cornelian in her hand and pressed it to her lips, kissing it all the time. Then she sent the maidens away, for she did not want them to know anything about the cornelian. They had seen her kiss it, but they did not know why she had done so.

That night she told all to the daughter of King Armanos, and, as soon as it was day, she sent for the captain of the ship and asked him about the merchant who owned the olives. From what the captain said, Princess Badoura felt sure that he was her own prince.

" Go at once," said she to the captain, "and bring him to me. He owes me some money, and if you fail to bring him you shall pay for it with your head."

The captain at once set off, and when he reached the city where Prince Camaralzaman lived he lost no time in going to the garden. He took with him some strong men, who seized the prince and dragged him by force to the ship. Not a word did they say as to why they acted so.

With a fair voyage the Isle of Ebony was reached, and no sooner did Princess Badoura know that the ship had cast anchor in the harbour than she went down to it.

Then once more she fell into the arms of her dear prince, and when her tears of joy were over she led him to the palace. It did not take long to tell the king all about their strange lives, and when he heard it he laughed with all his might.

Then, taking leave of King Armanos, the prince and princess set out for their own land. As king and queen they had a long and happy reign.

THE STORY OF PRINCE ZEYN ALASNAM AND THE KING OF THE GENII

THERE was once a King of Balsora who was very rich and good, and much loved by all the people whom he ruled. He had one son, whose name was Zeyn Alasnam, which means a beautiful statue. The king was very pleased when this little boy was born. Gathering together all the wise men in his country, he asked them to find out what sort of a boy the young prince would be. So the wise men went out into the palace garden on a fine starlit night, and, looking up at the stars, said they could see wonderful things that would happen to Prince Zeyn.

"The stars say he will be very brave," said one wise man. "They tell me that he will have strange adventures," said another. "And he will live to be very old," added a third.

The king was glad to hear that his son would be brave, because he thought all princes ought to have plenty of courage. He was also pleased to hear that he would have wonderful adventures, because they would show the people how very brave their prince could be.

The young prince grew up, and was taught everything that princes ought to know; but when he was still quite young, his father was taken very ill. Knowing that he was going to die, he sent for Prince Zeyn, and making him sit down by his side, talked to him seriously.

"You will soon be the king of this country," he said. "And I hope you will be a good one, whom your people will love. Do not listen to those who are always praising you, and try to find out the real truth before you punish any one."

Prince Zeyn promised to remember his father's words, and soon afterwards the old king died. For eight days the prince did nothing but weep for his father's death; but on the ninth he had to begin to govern; so he sat upon his father's throne and tried to rule instead.

At first, Zeyn was not a good king. Being able to do whatever he liked, he spent most of his time in amusing himself and spending money. His mother, a very wise queen, reminded him of his father's words, telling him that he would soon have no money left; and he began to feel sorry that he was not a better king, whom his people could love as they had loved his father.

But his money was all spent, and, not knowing where to get any more, he felt sad, and wished he had not spent it. One night he had a wonderful dream. He looked up and saw an old man standing beside his bed, and smiling kindly down upon him.

"Oh, Zeyn," said the old man, "joy comes after sorrow and happiness after sadness. If you want to be happy and rich again, get up and go to Cairo."

Prince Zeyn did not know what this meant, but in the morning he told his mother, who laughed at his dreams.

"Why do you laugh?" said Zeyn seriously. "The old man spoke very kindly. I believe he came to me in a dream to help me. He must be a kind of fairy, and I am going to obey him."

So, leaving the country to his mother's care, Zeyn crept out of his palace in the dark when nobody knew, and set off alone to Cairo. He arrived at the famous city, and feeling tired, lay down to sleep at the door of a mosque. There he had another wonderful dream. The old man coming again, told him to go straight home, as he would find the riches in his own palace.

Zeyn, angry at going on such a long journey for nothing, resolved to take no more notice of his dreams. When he told his mother, she did not laugh, but tried to comfort him. "If God wishes you to have riches, he will give them to you," she said. "Be a good king and, you will be a happy one."

But the first night after his return to his palace at Balsora the old man came again to Prince Zeyn in a dream. "The time of your riches has come," he said. "To-morrow morning, take an axe, and dig in your father's room. There you will find a great treasure."

Now Zeyn did not believe this, but, feeling

rather curious, he told the queen his dream, and then, sending for an axe, shut himself up alone in his father's room. He dug up the pavement until he was quite tired, but at last his axe struck against a white stone, which he lifted eagerly.

To his surprise, he found a door fastened with a padlock. The axe soon broke this, and there, before the prince, a marble staircase went down into the earth. Lighting a taper, Zeyn ran down, to find himself in a fine chamber with a crystal floor. All round it were four shelves, and on each shelf ten big urns.

Zeyn took off the lid of the first urn, and found it full of gold. He then looked into the other urns, and behold, every one was full of gold. He took a handful to the queen, who, greatly astonished, begged him not to waste them, and then they both went to the room where the treasure was hidden.

In one corner the queen saw another little urn, and inside it was nothing but a key. "This must lead to another treasure," they said, and, looking round the room, found a lock in the middle of the wall, which the key just fitted. When it was turned, this door opened, and showed a large hall in which stood eight shining diamond statues upon eight large gold pedestals.

But there was one more pedestal which had no statue, and above it lay a piece of white satin on which Zeyn read these words written by his father: "My dear son, all these statues are for you.

Go to Cairo, and find an old slave of mine, called Mobarec. He will show you a place where you may find a ninth statue more beautiful than all the rest."

When he had read this, Zeyn set off to discover a ninth statue to fill the empty pedestal. Going to Cairo, he soon found the old slave Mobarec, who was one of the richest men in the city, and lived in a large and beautiful house. Zeyn knocked at the door, and was taken into a large hall, where his father's old servant was sitting.

"I am the son of the King of Balsora," said Zeyn.

"I did not know he had a son. How old are you?" asked Mobarec.

"I am twenty years of age," replied the young prince.

"And how shall I know that you are speaking the truth?" said the old slave, looking straight into Zeyn's eyes.

"Because I can tell you that my father had a secret room in which were ten urns full of gold and eight diamond statues. I have come to you to ask you where to find the ninth," Prince Zeyn spoke in a loud voice, and Mobarec knelt at his feet. "You are indeed the young prince," he cried, "and must come to a great feast which I am giving to-day."

The next morning, Zeyn asked Mobarec if they could not set out on their search for the ninth statue. The old slave was quite ready, but said that the prince must be prepared to face many dangers. Now, as Zeyn was longing for adventures, this did not frighten him, and they set out together.

After travelling for many days they came to some tall and waving palm trees, standing all around a lake of shining water. A silver moon looked through the trees, and everything was very silent.

"You will now need all your courage," whispered Mobarec. "We are near the dreadful place where the ninth statue is guarded. We shall have to cross this water."

"But we have no boat," answered Zeyn.

"Wait a moment," said Mobarec, "and a fairy boat belonging to the king of the genii will appear. But, however strange it looks, be very careful not to make a sound. If you speak to the boatman we shall all go to the bottom and be drowned."

Mobarec shaded his eyes and looked across the shining water. In a moment a little boat came into sight with an amber mast and a floating sail of blue satin. The boatman was very strange to look at, for he had an elephant's head and a tiger's body. He did not speak, but, taking up Mobarec and Zeyn with his trunk, lifted them into the boat. In a moment they had crossed the lake, the only sound being the soft rush of oars in the water.

"We may speak now," said Mobarec. "We are on a beautiful island belonging to the king of the genii. Do you hear the birds singing, and see the wonderful colour of the fruit?"

Zeyn was delighted with everything, and very soon they came in front of an emerald castle with a golden gate, where several tall genii stood on guards. They were the fairies who lived on the island, and were tall and terrible to look at to those who did not understand them. But Mobarec did; so he took from under his robe two little square carpets, one for Zeyn, and one for himself. These were magic carpets, and those who sat on them were quite safe.

"The king of the genii will be here soon now," said Mobarec. "If he is angry with us for coming, he will look like a monster; but if he is pleased, he will be very handsome."

There was a flash of lightning, a loud noise of thunder, and then all the island went dark. A great crash sounded everywhere, and suddenly a big, fine-looking man stood before them, and began to smile.

"Welcome, Prince Zeyn," he said. "I loved your father, and whenever he came to see me, I gave him a diamond statue for his very own. It was I whom you saw in your dreams, and I promised your father to give you the ninth statue, which is the most beautiful of all.

"But there is only one way to get it. You must search the world until you find a beautiful maiden, who is not only clever, but who has never in her life spoken an angry word, or thought

a wicked thought. When you have found her,
bring her back here, to wait upon my queen, and
then I will give you the statue."

Zeyn promised to do all this, though he knew it
would be a hard task; but he asked the king of
the genii how he should know the maiden.

"I confess," replied the king, "that you will find
it hard, but here is a magic mirror. Only
the right maiden will be able to see her face in
this."

So Mobarec and Prince Zeyn went away into the
world again to find a perfect maiden. They
gathered together all the beautiful girls in Cairo,
but not one of them could see her own face in the
mirror. It grew dark and clouded whenever they
looked into it. They next went to Baghdad, where
they made friends with an old man named
Muezin, who told them that he knew the most
perfect maiden in the world.

She lived with her father, who had once been a
great man at the king's court, but who now spent
all his time teaching his daughter to be clever and
good. Muezin took Prince Zeyn to see her, and
when her father heard that he was the son of the
King of Balsora, he was very pleased to see him,
and at once allowed his daughter to look into the
magic mirror.

The moment she did so, she saw her own lovely
face in the shining glass, and every one standing
round saw it too. Zeyn had found the perfect
maiden that he sought. Now there was only one

way for him to get the maiden, and that was to marry her. Zeyn was quite ready to do this, for she was so good and so beautiful that he already loved her. Indeed, he found it very hard to keep his promise, and take her back to the king of the genii. He thought he would rather have the perfect maiden than the ninth statue.

There was a grand wedding, and Prince Zeyn and his bride set out from her father's house. They travelled for many days, and at last they came again to the shining water and the island where the king of the genii lived. Then the maiden, finding out that she was to be not a queen but a slave, wept bitterly, and begged to go home again. She thought that Prince Zeyn and Mobarec were very cruel, not seeing how sad they looked when they gave her up to the genii. The king of the magic island was very pleased with the maiden, and said she would be a beautiful slave for his queen. Then he turned to Prince Zeyn and said, "I am quite satisfied with all you have done. Go home now, and when you reach your palace at Balsora, go down at once into the room where the eight diamond statues are. There you will find the ninth statue, standing on its own pedestal."

Prince Zeyn was surprised to hear this, but, knowing he must obey the king of the genii, he went sadly home with Mobarec, leaving his lovely bride behind him. As soon as he reached the palace he told his mother all that had happened, and she was delighted to hear he would so soon have the ninth statue.

"Come, my son," she said, "let us both go down and look for the new treasure."

Together they went through the stone door, and down the marble staircase. They came to the diamond statues, and there Prince Zeyn stood still in surprise and delight. For the ninth statue was not made of diamonds or gold; it was the beautiful and perfect maiden whom he loved and whom he had been so sad to leave.

She stepped down from the pedestal, and Prince Zeyn was running to meet her, when there was a loud noise of thunder, and the king of the genii appeared.

"The ninth statue is your bride, Zeyn," he cried. "I have given her back to you, because you kept your promise."

The queen and all the court soon loved the perfect maiden almost as much as Zeyn himself, and he and she lived happily together until they were very old.